A Pirates

Booty

Book 2 of the Spacefaring Buccaneer Series

By W W Dowd III

A Pirates Booty

Books by WW Dowd:

Epik Adventure Series:
Here Be Dragons
Here Be Heroes
Here Be Evil

The Spacefaring Buccaneer Series
Birth of a Corsair
A Pirates Booty
The Captains Share

Cookbooks
The Dowd Family Cookbook – 2018
The Family Cookbook – 2020

Stories for the Campfire

Coming Soon: (Well as soon as I can finish writing them. So many stories, so little time)

The Spacefaring Buccaneer Series
Gauntlet*
Going Legit*

Single Books:
Soulshorn*
(Horror)
Dr. Zenier*
(Horror)
The Darker Side (Horror)

Western Tales Series:
Chahakta*

A Pirates Booty

*Riding for the
Brand**
*Bounty
Hunter**
Longshot*
*Leather and
Lead**

**Infernal
Blessings
Series:**
*Bound by
Darkness**
*Righteous
Anomalies**
*The Horror of
Beauty**
*Adventures in
Ennui**

**The Elders
Series:**
The Dowd*
*Medicine
Woman**
War Torn*

**Epik
Adventure
Series:**

*There Be
Monsters**
*There be
Madness**
*There Be
Magic**
There Be Gold*
There Be War*

*Forthcoming

4

Copyright © 2020 by WW Dowd
Published in the United States
by Stories by Bill
Hardcover ISBN:
Paperback ISBN:
9798552751723
EBook ISBN:
General Edit by: Lil Sami
Cover Concept: WW Dowd
Cover Polish: WW Dowd

Dedication

This book I would like to dedicate to Stephen, Terri, and Rashaun. I always appreciate the reminder that there are good, solid men and women out there. They are just hard to find because they are too busy working and taking care of business to draw attention to themselves. Roll on my friends. My classmates also deserve recognition, Gaylon, Robert, Micah, and Jack. One and done Baybee!

I also must mention Scott. Scott you are my favorite fan I have never met. Your excitement as you talk about these stories reminds me of why I write. I may never be a millionaire (or even a hundred thousand-aire) with my writing, but if these stories bring excitement and joy to people reading them, I am ecstatic. Thank you, Scott, for reading my stories and letting me know how much you enjoy them.

I also cannot get the image of a 6'6" man jumping up and down while squealing with delight out of my head… That is your fault Stephen.

Contents

Spacefaring Buccaneer Series

A Pirates Booty

Spacefaring Buccaneer Series

Chapter 1 – A Pirate Captain

Captain Jax – The Jack Ketch – Between the Milky Way Galaxy and Andromeda

The debris from the recent astronomical battle floated through space at the edge of the Milky Way galaxy in clouds of metallic detritus. Random bursts of energy spewed from the torn chunks of what were once space defying starships like the dying call of mortally wounded beasts hoping for salvation.

12

There was no salvation to be had in this empty sector of space for the enemies of the freedom rebellion. Labeled as pirates by the races of the Milky Way, the freedom rebellion had traversed the galaxy in hopes of that most elusive of desires… freedom. Unfortunately, freedom never came free, but had to be paid for with the blood of those willing to fight for the privilege.

Just to get to this point many had paid that ultimate price. Before true freedom could be had, many more would throw themselves into the meat grinder of war. Some things were worth fighting for; some things had to be fought for.

Jax watched the screen looking for signs of life amongst

the torn and burning metal. He knew the odds of finding survivors were awfully close to nil, but he refused to take the chance on even one of his people being left behind to die cold and alone as they drifted through space.

They were his people.

A deceptively soft contralto spoke close to his ear. "Jax we should go now. We searched as much of the wreckage as we can. We rescued everyone possible." Jax's executive officer, life mate, best friend, and most trusted ally Allie, placed a hand gently on his shoulder as she spoke. She could be the hardest woman Jax had ever known but at times like these she revealed her softer side to him. The side no one else ever saw. The side she had hidden away since becoming one of Arrex Ten's new cyborg series.

Jax almost wished he could kill Arrex all over again for what it had done to them.

Wiping his hand over his face as if he could clean off the horrors he had seen, the horrors he himself had been required to perform, Jax turned to her. "You are right Allie. Gather the prisoners in the shuttle bay aboard the *Gold Digger* and let Captain Drake know we will be over in a half hour to discuss terms of surrender."

For just a moment Allie showed surprise before schooling her face into the scowl she wore when others were around. "Terms? You mean they have choices?"

A Pirates Booty

Jax sighed before responding. "Yes Allie. We all have choices. In the universe we live in now they are rarely good choices though."

With a quick nod Allie moved to contact Captain Drake before leaving to round up the prisoners aboard the *Jack Ketch* to transport them to the much larger *Gold Digger*.

As she left the bridge Jax wondered how he had ever been talked into taking Captainship of the *Jack Ketch* and now fleet captain of their small mixed group. Now he had to decide how to deal with the prisoners. He couldn't let them go take knowledge of his people back, but he knew the torment of the indent control methods the corporations used. Like he had told Allie, there were rarely any good choices anymore.

When he entered the shuttle bay of the *Gold Digger* Jax could see the obvious signs of the recent battle. Against one wall a mangled shuttle lay half fused with the framework, still sparking occasionally in its death throes. Jax could only hope someone had deemed it safe for now, since no one worked to clear it. With a grim chuckle he guessed that a mere shuttle wreck in the launch bay didn't rate emergency repairs. Seared and bent framework with scarred and torn plates completed the ravaged décor. No one was wearing environment suits or armor, so they must have

17

repaired the bay enough to kept in atmosphere.

Jax simply opened his visor rather than take off his helmet, no need to take chances when he didn't have to.

Standing to one side Drake, Baylee, Maddie and Allie awaited his approach. They looked as worn as he felt. Captain Drake, and Allie, friends since the beginning of this nightmare, stood with military stiffness while Jax's sister Baylee stood beside Drake with one arm around his waist. Captain Maddie stood talking around a cigar as big as roll of quarters. None looked up as Jax approached. This could be a dirty business and they were each happy Jax would be the one making these decisions. Avoiding

18

having to think about what he might need to do, Jax scowled a moment as he thought of the stress to the damaged air recyclers from Captain Maddie's cigar. Of course, how much added work was one cigar when the recyclers had to deal with millions of cubic feet of atmosphere filled with the smoke of countless fires and chemical leaks? Jax decided in the scheme of things the cigar remained a non-issue, certainly not enough to warrant an argument with the Captain of the *Kraken* about.

May as well get this over with. "How many?" Jax used his command tone. This was not a duty to be casual about.

Captain Drake of the newly christened *Gold Digger* stepped

19

forward. "Over two hundred so far, but we have more coming."

"We best get on with it. Where is Dr. Claudeburge?" Jax asked as he kept a military stance. "We need him to verify answers."

A golf ball looking enviro suit zipped into the bay announcing the arrival of Hed. The alien promach could not withstand the pressure required for human comfort. To be able to interact with humans and gharians, the promach required a separate environmentally protected vehicle. Sometimes Jax envied him that.

Sound emitted from the vehicle, though no discernable speaker could be identified.

"The waste of skin that is Dr. Claudeburge claims he is too

busy in med bay and asked me to perform his duties, as if I had nothing better to do."

Jax sighed as he mentally prepared himself to interrogate the prisoners and hopefully separate the ones that were honestly willing to join his fledgling crew. This promised to be a very long day indeed. Squaring his shoulders Jax gave the order. "Bring forth the first prisoner."

The first detainee brought before him turned out to be a human cyborg named Noah. Adorned in ratty white coveralls, his clothes looked like they had been printed months ago. Signs of abuse and malnutrition covered what skin showed and his eyes had the haunted look Jax had come to associate with the soul crushing defeatism of a life term 1A indents. How could Jax sentence a man like this? The only thing he was truly guilty of was being born in a universe bent on his destruction. Jax had to clear his throat before speaking.

"What do you have to say for yourself prisoner?" The words sounded cold even to his own ears. What choice did he have though? Freedom had yet to be a reality and hard choices would have to be made.

The prisoner Noah looked Jax in the eye for just a moment before dropping his head to stare at the floor again. "Your golf ball thing done took out the control software. For that I thank you. I never dreamed I would ever experience a free mind again. I go to my maker a free man. That is more than I could ever have hoped for."

Jax shouldn't have been surprised by the words. Synth controlled their indents through software hardwired directly into their brain. In fact, Drake, Allie and himself had been similarly shackled. Stepping closer to the prisoner Jax commanded. "Look up. Look me in the eye. How do you feel about fighting with us? You would never have to bow your head again…"

The look of hope tore Jax's heart more than he cared to admit.

"Freedom and a chance to fight back? I don't see the question here." Noah's face screwed up as if he feared to even hope.

Still facing the prisoner Jax called to Hed, "Well, what do you say?"

Hed grumped in normal Hed fashion. "Yeah, Yeah. The prisoner is telling the truth, for now anyway. Kind of a miserable specimen if you ask me though."

And so it went over two hundred times.

Chapter 2 – Failure Is Not an Option

Peadee Five – PD-395 Carrier Squadron –Shepard Spur – Milky Way Galaxy

The central core of the Combined PD-395 carrier squadron held one of the most complex blends of hardware and software in the known universe.

It held one of the shadows of Peadee Five, ancient of the Synth Lord peoples.

Peadee Five kept his essence in several systems, a security measure most of the synth lords adhered to. The Synth Lords kept very stringent security. Not only did they make enemies of other species, Synth Lords often fought amongst each other, battles that could, and sometimes did, destroy entire solar systems.

Even so, the community stayed small since few synth lords created new life in their ranks. Creating progeny often created new enemies. Very few familial obligations existed in synth society. The entire robotic species survived because their lives spanned millennium. Peadee Five itself had been conscious for over five thousand years, witnessing the rise of several biological species to spacefaring status. Peadee had been amongst the first of the synth lords to guide the new entries into their proper place in the galactic order.

A place deemed appropriate by the Synth council. i.e. slaves.

All of this mattered only because of the situation at hand. Synth lords died when caught by galactic events, such as supernovas or black hole density changes. Sometimes synth lords died in battle with another synth lord.

In Peadee Fives long eidetic memory, no synth had ever been destroyed by a biological, ever. It simply wasn't possible, yet a small group of meat sacks had managed to kill Arrex Ten. Arrex's own indents had performed the heinous deed! Not even subversive indents sent by another synth had killed Arrex.

A Pirates Booty

No specialized hardware or synth
level backup to a masterfully
executed plan. Just biologicals
acting haphazardly, as biologicals
did. Biologicals acting with little
planning and even less intellect.
The whole thing went against the
basic laws of the universe. Peadee
Five could only acknowledge that
the laws of universal chaos had
focused directly on RX01 for
something like this to happen.

Arrex Ten, the only progeny
Peadee had created in the
millenniums of its existence.
Arrex had been slated as a better
version with better analytics and
logic systems. Peadee tried to
reason to itself that Arrex had
only been a few hundred years
old and had not developed the
experience to properly create his
security systems. Arrex had been

naïve and foolish, interacting
with the meat sacks much more
often than prudent, becoming
vulnerable to just such
randomized chaos. Perhaps it
was best that Arrex Ten had been
removed from the exalted ranks
of the synth lords prior to other
synth lords realizing its
substandard engineering. Peadee
Five had a reputation to
maintain. Any progeny Peadee
created directly reflected on
Peadee itself.

Arrex Ten might have been
an abject failure. Even so such an
action from the biologicals
required consequences.
Consequences so dire that none
would ever entertain the thought
of action against the synth lords
again.

A Pirates Booty

But first Peadee had to find the biologicals that had performed the heinous deed. Peadee could have just taken vengeance against the species, wiping them from the universe like a roach infestation.

It wasn't like he hadn't shoved a species into extinction before, starting so very long ago against the biologicals that didn't understand just what they had created in the synth lords. Peadee recalled the violence of that era fondly, often bringing the memories forward as a soothing balm to remind himself of the savage joy of the era. That was before the synth concluded that biologicals could be useful. Before the synth council agreed that using the biologicals as slaves held a much higher efficiency rating. Before the synth had attained the status of chess masters over all other sentient species.

The meat species even enslaved themselves, leaving the synth lords to simply order what they required for a few baubles and some very low-grade tech. The system worked well for all concerned.

Until now.

Not only had this group extinguished Arrex Ten, but they had done so using synth lord technology. Three of them contained synth lord technology embedded into the meat sack of their physical body.

If Arrex wasn't dead already, Peadee would have killed it for being such an idiot.

A Pirates Booty

Now a significant amount of Peadee Five's resources headed to the Andromeda Galaxy on the trail of the miscreants to exact a terrible, and very public retributon, synth lord style.

Had Peadee been able to smile it would have been grinning when two of his own enhanced biologicals stepped into the audience room Peadee had chosen for direct interaction with his minions. Peadee didn't require such interaction since it could directly send commands to their implants, but it enjoyed the terror the biologicals emitted during the process. Peadee liked to think of these meetings as an affectation it deserved to indulge in.

"Report," the communicator barked at the two.

Simultaneously Peadee sent
subtle direct commands to their
embedded chips enhancing the
subordinates' terror.

Both meat sacks knew better
than succumbing to the
terrorizing effects. Standing stiff
as a board they responded
crisply. "Cyber enhanced units
Phelan and Carmen reporting
your lordship. The prey now
moves toward the Andromeda
galaxy with three starships. A
human military destroyer, a grain
carrier, and a prototype vessel
not in the registry to be precise.
Their signal is faint and will
disappear to our own sensors
within the hour if we do not
pursue immediately. Even then
we will lose the signal before we
can match speeds. The starships

are damaged and two are older models so we should be able to overtake them relatively quickly. The prototype vessel may be a bit more challenging to capture should it follow the intelligent course and leave the others behind."

Evan as he relished the meat bags terror Peadee responded, "You are human. What do you believe they plan?"

The two cyborgs hesitated for over seven hundred milliseconds. Incorrect answers invariably proved to be painful. Phelan blurted out his conjecture before Peadee considered the hesitation unresponsiveness. "If it were me in those ships I would be running as fast and as far as I could to live out my life in constant dread of being found. Running and hiding would be the best option such an inferior being could take."

Carmen babbled out her response defensively. "I believe they will attempt to lay a trap to fight back. They have already shown their insanity in attacking one of your excellencies people. They have already signed their own death warrant; in their madness they may believe they have a chance of victory."

Even the body control systems both cyborgs had installed could not stop the trickles of sweat beginning to runnel down their faces. By the time Peadee answered the room stank of fear. Peadee relished the free borne particles his sensors picked up from the two. It allowed the silence to linger heavy in the air before it spoke.

"So, you say they will follow a fight or flight scenario? I could have found such rudimentary information on a human psychology primer. All earthborn creatures subscribe to fight or flight tactics when threatened. I am disappointed in your service, but do not worry. I will give you a chance to redeem yourself in my eyes. For now, you must be reminded of the results of poor performance."

Peadee could activate every single pain center while keeping each muscle taut through a few simple commands to their enhancement control unit. Peadee did just that. The two meat sacks could not even scream through throat muscles held tight. They tried though. Peadee watched them as their eyes widened and leaked fluid. Moment later they expelled fluids into their cloth coverings. Peadee wondered at a species so ashamed of its meat that it kept constantly coated in cloth. No matter, the cloth stank from the bodily expulsions and would need to be replaced after cleansing the meat sacks. Peadee sent an order to have the two taken to the chem lab to be scrubbed clean. As the two were carried away they attempted feeble protests but Peadee saw no reason to listen. Sometimes he enjoyed his interactions with humans very much indeed.

During cleansing the screams lasted longer than the vocal

cords. Peadee loved the wracking
sobs best anyway.

Chapter 3 – Intellect and Emotions

Allie – The Jack Ketch – Outer Edge of the Milky Way Galaxy

Allie sat in the storage cubicle spinning old fashioned coins between her fingers. The glittering disks spun faster than most people could follow but that was a sign of her nervousness. Well, if she was going to be truly honest with herself, spinning four coins at once would have been impossible before she had 'enhancements' surgically implanted. Enough changes had been made to her human body that she technically wasn't considered fully human anymore. She was human enough though. Human enough for Jax and that was all that mattered to her. With everything that had been going on she held to that one guiding beacon. No matter how bad things got, Jax would always be there by her side.

Unfortunately, he had the insight of Andromedin swamp moss, and this screwed up idea that he needed to help people. That would be fine, Allie could live with that, except Jax also held a gold medal in poor character judgement. The poor dirt kicking sod trusted absolutely the wrong sorts of people. People like that bimbo that made all the cooing noises and kept touching Jax's shoulder and pressing against him with more familiarity than any crew member should. Why with one hand Allie could…

She came out of her dark musings as the door slid open. Tossing aside the mangled coins she had inadvertently crumpled in irritation, she stood so fast she jumped a bit.

"You said you would be here at 17:30. It is now 17:32:25. You are late Baylee, and I have not seen Glixen or Hed yet. If we are to conspire against your brother, we cannot be so sloppy. He would not understand that we work for his own good".

"Settle down, Allie. I was researching the accords with Glixen. Glixen went to Hed to get a copy of the originals. They

41

should be here momentarily. And for the record, we are not conspiring. We are acting as the senior officers that we are and determining a strategic plan to avoid foreseen unpleasantness". Baylee was rather proud of the way the words flowed out smoothly, as if she hadn't prepared them just in case they were caught. Self-delusion or not, that was her story, and she was sticking to it.

"Ha!" Allie snorted, "If that is the case why are we meeting in a storage cubicle? You know how Captain Jax would react to this if he found out." Allie paced as she spoke, unconsciously adding the Captain prefix when speaking to others. Calling the Captain by his given name alone she saved for the privacy of her own thoughts, and the increasingly rare moments they were alone together.

"You wouldn't be here if you didn't agree with me. You know as well as I do the crew, human and alien, needs cohesiveness before we all self-destruct from the infighting. Glixen believes *ne* found a way to bring everyone together under Jax. I'll let *nem* explain it all when *ne* gets here".

The pronouns for the third cthichek sex called *nemales* still felt odd on Baylee's tongue. She fought through the language adjustment rather than call the crablike alien 'it'. To do otherwise just seemed rude.

"And that's another thing, why are we cozening up to aliens? They don't even think like we do! If we are to do this, can't we have allies that are at least human? Or cyborg? Glixen, worries me enough running all over the ship in that rolling tank of *nirs*. Hed wandering around in a floating golf ball can be even worse. You do realize outside of his micro ship Hed looks like a blob of snot, don't you? A jellyfish shaped glob of snot".

Baylee shook her head trying to keep a reasonable tone. Sometimes Allie could be a bit rough around the edges. "You don't mean that. Glixen and Hed were the ones that started this entire bid for freedom. Without them neither you, Drake, or Jax would have ever escaped Arrex Ten in the first place". Baylee's paramour Drake captained the *Gold Digger,* a rechristened

44

destroyer they had pirated, but all of that was another story, another worry. Baylee hoped they could pull this off. She relished the idea of real freedom with Drake and the idea of going back to a life of hopelessness scared the wits out of her. She refused to even contemplate the possibility.

Before Allie share a scathing retort, the door swished open again to allow in Drake and Ja'Zarha. Drake's cybernetic body stood a lean six foot and change but he looked almost petite beside the towering reptilian creature beside him. Ja'Zarha stood closer to ten feet than nine and weighed the best part of a full ton. Allie watched as he carefully drew in his tail before the door swished closed. Even standing in the same room as the gharian made Allie want to arm herself and lunge into battle.

Of course, Baylee slid quickly into Drakes arms as soon as he entered. They seemed so natural and comfortable Allie just wanted to slap them both. She shook her head. That was just jealousy raring its green-eyed alien head. Allie did like Baylee and Drake, just sometimes she wished they weren't so... exhibitionist in their affection.

Maybe she just wanted that kind of public display with Jax, she thought to herself introspectively. Emotions were complicated, life was simpler with emotions properly suppressed by the cybernetic software.

Allie snapped more harshly than she intended, "If you two are finished canoodling can we get down to business? I understand you have found a way to provide a focus point to bring the crew together and loyal to Jax. The longer we spent in this closet the more chance of having to explain to Jax what we intend. You know as well as I do, he won't like it."

Ja'Zhara spoke through his translator. "The cyborg is correct. Where are the others? Specifically, where are the caustic goop Hed and the little mother Glixen?" Ja'Zarha's voice came out as a sibilant growl. The gharians communicated with sound so the translator he wore adjusted his voice to galactic common, just as it translated the communication of others around into gharian standard for his audio organs. While Hed's rough way of speaking challenged the gharians to no end, the promise of offspring the cthichek Glixen had made gave *nir* almost revered status with the gharians.

Baylee turned to look up at the huge gharian. "That's the thing. Hed and Glixen are bringing copies of the original accords. We will go over that as soon as they get here."

Drake pulled away from Baylee, his visage gone suddenly serious as he addressed Allie. "Ja'Zhara and I have seen modified copies of the accords. Mainly the difference between what you are proposing and the

48

indenture of the Milky Way conglomerate."

For just a moment Allie's visage showed her ire before responding. "Well for a full explanation you would have to talk to your girlfriend instead of spending all of your time sucking face. Essentially, the difference is that we choose to enter the accord of our own free will and the bond cannot be transferred. The bond links us to Captain Jax and only Captain Jax. Indenture twisted the concept to unrecognizability. "

Ja'Zhara interjected with his rumbling voice. "I don't see why we would ever go back into slavery no matter the benefit. Hundreds of gharians have died for this chance at freedom, shall their lives be deemed wasted?"

Her body tensed in battle stance; Allie snapped a reply. "Perhaps you want baby lizards of your own? And you want said lacertilian snippets to have a chance at the freedom we never had? The infighting has already begun Ja'Zhara. At this rate we will never make across the deep black to Andromeda without imploding from infighting. We have to do something and Jax is the only creature aboard any of the ships that has even a snowballs chance in hell of being able to pull it together. But he can't or won't do it for himself That is why we are even here, to do what Jax is too stubborn to do himself."

Chastised, Ja'Zhara mumbled a response. "I don't know what frozen water and religious damnation have to do with anything, but I admit your point."

The swish of the door announced Hed and Glixen. The promach and the cthichek each sat within an armored environmental chamber designed for their individual species. Hed within what looked like a two-foot diameter floating golf ball, and Glixen in a tracked vehicle that resembled nothing so much as a twentieth century tank. Both species spoke through speakers from their translating system since their native form of communication consisted of pulses of light. This was one of the reasons communications could be difficult since any inflection in tone or language came from the translator's 'best guess' software.

Baylee redirected the question to Hed. "Ja'Zarha wants to know why he should go along with the plan to invoke the accords. Care to explain Hed?" She stood defiantly beside Drake. Though obviously intimidated by the huge gharian. Baylee refused to let it show. From Allies perspective she failed miserably.

There was no way to read Hed's expressions within the enclosure, which irritated Allie to no end, but even she had to admit he spoke with alacrity.

"Because we have developed a way to take your shame from you. All the gharians away from their home worlds have two things in common; they are all male; and they shall never be a part of the gharian familial structure. No gharian male sold into indenture has any connection to a lounge. We plan to change that." Hed's translator added a note of excitement to the words.

Ja'Zarha snapped back, "And how do you plan to do that? Take us back to Gharia and explain that we should get a second chance to compete for placement with a female's lounge? No gharian male has ever been able to compete twice in recorded history. But of course, they will make an exception for a wad of goop because he asked so nicely." Ja'Zarha snorted in disgust.

A Pirates Booty

Glixen had backed into the door. Allie didn't know if all cthichek strenuously avoided conflict or just "their" cthichek Glixen did, but it was truly annoying to deal with. Unlike his actions though, his words came from his translator decisively. "Of course not, Ja'Zarha. We plan to start a brand-new lounge consisting of our own gharians."

Ja'Zarha deflated a bit. "Yes. Yes. The Captain promised as much, but we have not found a suitable female."

Glixen responded almost immediately. "No need. I have enough DNA to develop the hatchlings to a healthy egg right here on the ship. The only question becomes how many hatchlings each of the gharians want versus our available resources."

At that point the argument began in earnest as the group divided up the available resources for their own ends. Allie watched each of the conspirators wondering for just a moment if they were making a huge mistake. Jax would be furious if he ever found out about her part in this. She could only hope that he would understand that even in this she worked to take care of him and forgive her without too much bluster. She refused to even think about what she would do if he decided she had truly betrayed him. She had watched him in the combat training area. She didn't think even she and Drake combined with their considerable enhancements could take Jax without all out lethal combat. All of this was for his own good though. She just had to keep telling herself that.

Allie held a hand up to forestall the arguments. "I have certain requirement I expect from this venture. I will not argue. These are nonnegotiable."

No reason Allie shouldn't make sure she had some say in the matter. From all she had read, women had given away their freedom for their men since time began. She for one refused to give hers up without making sure she got what she needed.

Chapter 4 – Not as Empty as Advertised

Jax – The Jack Ketch – Between the Milky Way Galaxy and Andromeda

The normally star jeweled view of space now had only the dusting of a few faint twinkles in the optics of the pirate ship the *Jack Ketch*. Though the smallest by tonnage of the three starships, the *Jack Ketch* could outrun or outfight either the modified grain hauler the *Kraken*, or the repurposed corporate destroyer the *Gold Digger*. The ragged trio of ships, too disparate and small to for such a grand designation as a flotilla or an armada, journeyed across the vast emptiness between galaxies in search of haven. And by haven they hoped for a planet to settle and perhaps even enjoy that elusive dream called freedom. Many had died just to get to this point and many more would likely feel the cold embrace of raw space before their journeys were complete.

Right now, the ships worked toward capturing a zenarplast. A little understood creature of deep space that produced power crystals by the thousands. These crystals could be used to fuel FTL engines used by all known species. Manufacturing these crystals remained the standard practice amongst shipping lines. The 'real deal' produced cleaner and more efficient power and thus spacers of all species avidly sought such bonanzas.

"Damnit Allie, you need to take out the central nerve bundle. Damage anywhere else costs us money!" Jax growled across the bridge of the *Jack Ketch*, his corvette class starship. He had to admit he like the sound of that. HIS starship. Who would have ever thought that he could become captain of his own starship? Though technically, he guessed the *Jack Ketch* was now a corsair class starship since he had stolen it and had plans to use his acquisition to raid the commerce of the Starburst Interstellar Transport Company. Assuming he could find a place to base out of, and survived the empty space between galaxies to get to Andromeda, and his crew didn't kill him outright in a mutinous coup, and…

His train of thought derailed by his First Mate's response, "If you think you can do better, you get over here and do it your own self, *Captain*. Why don't you tell Drake to take the *Gold Digger* for lead on this if you are so worried about it". Allie wasn't the type of woman, well cyborg, a man argued with for long. Not if a man wanted all his pieces to stay attached and in the same place anyway, and yet she was the best friend Jax had ever had; followed closely by the captain of the stolen and repurposed *Gold Digger*, Drake.

The three had met and become friend's years before their

purchase by Arrex the synth lord.
Their time with Arrex had been
hard on all three of them. Arrex
was the reason Jax, Allie, and
Drake no longer remained purely
human. After the "upgrades"
Arrex had installed, the
integrated hardware attendant to
the cybernetic suite had changed
their designation from human to
cyborg. Jax sometimes worried
about the possible loss of their
humanity, but that didn't mean
he was going to push matters by
arguing with Allie too much.

"You know the *Jack Ketch* is
faster and packs more of a punch
than the *Gold Digger*, but if you
don't feel up to the task..." Jax
dangled the bait in front of Allies
pride.

And he got a hit. "You need to drop that idea right now, Jax. There's not a ship made in the Milky Way that could harvest a zenarplast without destroying half the product or damaging themselves in the process. A few little strikes on the edges won't make any difference."

The three ships of the micro fleet Jax had scrabbled together had found the zenarplast moving along almost parallel to their line of travel hunting like a shark zoning in on bleeding fish. Zenarplast showed on sensors as an energy anomaly the size of most solar systems. While no one had come up with definitive proof that zenarplast fell within the classification of a living organism, everyone agreed they followed the energy emissions of

starships to absorb energy
expelled from explosions created
when the zenarplast broke down
the hull and engine core. Of even
more importance, zenarplast
bodies contained nodes encasing
the crystals that energized the
most powerful starship engine
chambers developed to date.
These crystals were also
impervious to the effects of faster
than light travel when set outside
shielding.

The result: these crystals
could be made through an
expensive process that yielded
only a few per year, or they could
be harvested by the thousands
from a zenarplast.

With Maddie waiting in the
Kraken with her pull crates only
half full, Jax had decided to go for

the unexpected opportunity. Even if they only received ten percent of value selling on the black market, the bonanza from the crystals could keep all three starships and their crews living like kings for decades.

Jax's sister Baylee interjected her own thoughts into the banter via the comm system. "Drake decided to give a hand. He's coming in on the flank Allie so watch your shots."

"Jax, tell that sorry excuse for a bag of parts I got this." Allie growled as the two main cannons finally came online. The *Jack Ketch* boasted an unparalleled array of armament for her size and class even without her experimental antimatter dissolution emitters. The entire starship design revolved around the slow, heavy weapons but they gave the *Jack Ketch* a powerful advantage in any kind of violent interaction. Assuming they had time to power up the things. From target acquisition to first salvo took a minimum of twelve minutes, even once the ADE system was fully online, the armament couldn't cycle faster than once every twelve seconds. In a space battle seconds felt like hours and minutes felt like days.

The forte of the system lay in the sheer destruction the deep ebon lances left in the wake of their five-foot diameter beams. Jax had heard of weapons on super dreadnoughts having something like it, but those starships had crews in the tens of thousands and were of a size comparable to the Earth's moon. The *Jack Ketch* ran a paltry 275-foot length with a normal crew of thirty. Now she carried fifty, but many of those were untrained gharians and humans freed from synth indenture. Gharians as a species looked a lot like long armed renditions of the old Godzilla vids, only 7 to 10 feet tall and capable of speech.

The bridge erupted in a cheer as Allie scored a perfect shot into the central nerve knot of the zenarplast. The cheers were short lived as the zenarplast spasmed out in its death throws, slamming the ship with waves of power that came close to overcoming the shielding. In this case, close wasn't good enough and Jax opened a commlink to the *Gold Digger* and the *Kraken*.

"All right everybody. We got nothing but time, let's make sure we get every crystal we can. Drake, you are going to have to go on auto pilot while your crew gathers the crystals. Maddie, send some crew from your personnel crate to give Drake a hand gathering. It's payday peoples. Let's not waste it."

Chapter 5 – Finding Home

Jax – The Jack Ketch – Between the Milky Way Galaxy and Andromeda

By the time the crew loaded the raw crystals into every nook and cranny the *Gold Digger* didn't have enough space for a full crew even had they had one. *The Kraken* printed out two more towing crates, taking a goodly portion of their ore supply, to stuff full of the rest of the gathered bonanza. The *Kraken* looked like a proper freighter with two crystal crates, two

personnel crates, a food base
crate, a now partially loaded ore
crate and an equipment crate in
tow as well as a Star Cutter and a
tug stolen from the Podunk
security force.   Since their small
armada had only begun to sail
across the vast gulf between the
Milky Way galaxy and the
Andromedin galaxy, the trip
looked to be a long and cramped
one. Drake had tried to talk Jax
into printing another cargo crate,
but Jax had denied the request.
Without knowing where their
next load of ore for the metal
printers would come from, he felt
they needed to be as frugal as
possible with what they had.

Now Jax looked at the star
charts he had available for the
Andromeda galaxy. So much

information on the maps remained unsubstantiated he wasn't sure they were even worth looking at. He had to decide soon though. They were coming to a point that they required a specific point to navigate to. Moving generally toward Andromeda wasn't an effective option anymore. The most obvious planets had outposts from the corporations and the governments of the Milky Way which would react violently to the presence of free ships from back home. Freedom and the Milky Way governments didn't blend well. Of course, they might be a little upset with the fact that all three starships in their entourage were technically stolen.

When he had first
recommended escaping to
Andromeda the nebulous concept
had been exciting, but the reality
was that they could spend years
just looking for a planet that fell
within acceptable parameters for
their needs. Everyone expected
Jax to pull an answer out of his
pocket and his pockets remained
empty of ideas.

When the entry chimed Jax
jumped up, glad for the
distraction. Rather than call for
the guest to enter he walked over
to the door and opened it to find
a tracked and armored
environmental vehicle with a
turret that sported what Jax had
to guess was a heavy assault
cannon. The vehicle was only
four feet high, three wide and six

long, but had to weigh over ten tons. Jax again appreciated the Black hole plate used for the decking in the Jack Ketch. The vehicle rolled across the floor plates without leaving a scratch.

Waving a hand casually over his shoulder Jax motioned to an open space in the room. "Com'on in Glixen. How may I help you?"

Glixen was a member of the cthichek species. A crab looking species with an exoskeleton as well as an internal skeleton. Cthichek could live comfortably in environments that would kill all the other species in seconds. From the frozen cold and pressure of ammonia oceans storming across super gas giants to floating asteroids in space, cthichek built homes and thrived making a name for themselves as

top rated engineers. Cthichek
were also the only species
capable of surviving the
foundries used in making black
hole compressed metals, such as
the black hole steel used on all
starships.

The tracked vehicle
maneuvered to the indicated
open space and settled before
speaking. The voice of the
translator came out as a deep
smooth baritone with a hint of an
eastern accent.

"I hope I do not interrupt
your day Captain Jax. If so, I will
come back later." Glixen began
obsequiously.

"No Glixen. If fact I don't
mind any excuse to get away
from what I was working on." Jax

turned off the star maps as he spoke.

"That was a star map of Andromeda." The rich baritone emitted from the air in front of the tracked suit.

"Yes, Glixen. I am still deciding where we want to start our search for a place to settle and base our operations from. Everything on the front edge has outposts we want to avoid, and the interior areas do not have good data on them". Jax set his hands palm down on his desk to keep from fidgeting. Glixen often took physical cues incorrectly so the best way to interact often meant not to move any more than necessary.

"I have heard of a place from the crew. They said it would be an excellent place to begin out search". A holographic star map came into existence in front of Glixen. "They say this system would be very profitable".

Jax brought up the large star map of Andromeda then zoomed in to the area Glixen spoke of. A dual star system with over twenty planets in a complicated orbit between the two had as good a chance as any to yield what they were looking for. He did not like the black hole only a few light years from the system though. That had to play havoc with the systems balance of gravity, not to mention making navigation to the site challenging to say the least.

"I don't know Glixen. Navigating into that mess might be more than we want to start out with. There are so many competing gravity wells that we could skew off course without being prepared for it. Unless there is a significant reason to start there, I can't see the risk being worth the possible gain". Jax tried to emote understanding, but he had no clue just how much Glixen understood from *nir* translators physical cue software.

"I myself understand completely captain, but the cthichek crew really wants to start there. Of course, I myself will go wherever you lead us". Jax could hear a note of pleading in *nir* voice even as he fought to remember the proper pronouns for the third sexed cthichek. He, him, his, his and himself for males; She, her, her, hers and herself for females; Ne, nem, nir,

76

nirs, and nemself for nemales, the third sex of the cthichek. Jax just had to focus to remember the proper pronouns. Even talking to another species could be frustrating if you weren't careful of meanings.

"Okay Glixen, which crew are asking to go there and why? I can't just harry us across the universe on a whim".

"All of the Cthichek wish to go there. And should one of them mention that it would be the best place to raise young gharian hatchlings developed for the males I am certain the gharians will also ask that we go there. Much more forcibly than the Cthichek would since they are a very emotional and violent species.

77

A Pirates Booty

Glixen had fulfilled a promise he had made to the gharian contingent of the crew by developing gharian zygotes for each of them. A gharians entire existence revolved around the need for progeny. The social interactions as well as customs of the Gharians as a species revolved around this basic need. The Gharians working in space were all castoffs who had failed to win a family on their home planet. To have a family to care for after having gone through the shame of being deemed unfit for reproduction rendered the onboard gharians fanatical in their desire for progeny.

The idea of nine-foot reptiles with four-inch claws and a mace like tail pissed off because he wouldn't go where they needed to go for the good of their progeny didn't exactly give Jax the warm and fuzzies.

"Glixen, you are one of only two cthichek on all three ships. Are you threatening to get the Gharians all worked up over this?" Jax could hardly believe what he was hearing. Jax didn't know about other cthichek, but Glixen avoided anything remotely resembling confrontation. For him to attempt, albeit poorly, to blackmail Jax with the Gharians showed more aggression than he had ever heard of from a cthichek. Going to that planet must be important. Not to mention that since Glixen had agreed to develop the eggs for the gharians they practically

79

worshipped *nem*. By having progeny, the gharians could once again claim familial honor and the gharians in his crew had taken the patronym Ja' to show they were of the family of the freedom clan. That whole situation was another can of worms Jax would have to deal with, another day.

"No captain I would do no such thing. In fact, I would offer myself, my life and my freedom as assurance that I am totally loyal to you". The words came out oddly formal for a translated sentence.

That stunned Jax. "We just got free of slavery Glixen! Why would you offer yourself so quickly into slavery all over again?"

The tracks of the environmental vehicle rocked back and forth, a trait Jax had learned meant Glixen was becoming nervous. "You humans, erm, cyborgs, do not understand cthichek habits." Glixen said referring to Jax's enhancement courtesy of the synth lord Arrex. "We cthichek do not require freedom. We require security and safety. I offer myself to you knowing you will not damage me without good cause. You may fight for freedom, but I fight for safety. The synth lord Arrex was much too unstable and careless of his slaves and often killed them for no good reason. I have yet to see you throw away the life of a subordinate when you did not have to. Ergo you are safer as my master than Arrex could ever have been. The cthichek aboard this ship feel so strongly I will make the full declaration here and now".

Jax didn't know what to say to Glixen's declaration. He tried to explain. "Glixen you can follow without being a slave. That is what choice is all about. Making decisions for yourself".

Suddenly the room flashed in colored lights blinking furiously atop the turret of Glixen's vehicle. The translated voice took on an ominous note. "Formally and without reservation I, Glixen of the Fromage Cthichek declare *(No translation)* upon the person of Captain Jax of the *Jack Ketch*. This formal declaration supersedes all others and denies the right to make new declaration without specificity from all parties. I, Glixen of Fromage Cthichek pronounce *(No translation)* y Captain Jax. May the union *(No Translation).*

Jax had no clue how to react. Heck, he didn't even know what the cthichek Glixen had just declared or even if it was a declaration. He could feel his mouth working but nothing came out. How did you respond when even the translation software couldn't translate what Glixen was saying? Jax had a terrible suspicion that whatever Glixen had just imparted had consequences he might never understand.

"Well, uhm, if it is that important to you, we can go to

that system Glixen, there is no
need for all this". Jax tried to
steady his voice as he ran a hand
through his hair. The stray
thought that his hair was longer
than it had been his whole adult
life impinged the moment. A lot
of things had changed, many not
nearly as innocuous as freedom
to grow your hair as you chose.

"It was not I that made the
demand, but the will of the
cthichek crew. You have accepted
(No translation). They are
satisfied".

Jax started to argue that there
was only two cthichek crew so
any interaction with the cthichek
crew would likely be with *nem*
since Jax had never interacted
with the other cthichek and likely
wouldn't since the other cthichek
now resided on the *Gold Digger*.

Breathing a deep sigh Jax gave up. He would not change the way Glixen refused to accept responsibility in a single day. He just wished he knew what Glixen had just promised as well as what had just transpired.

Running his hand over his face Jax attempted to change the subject. "So, uhm, Glixen. How are the gharian eggs looking?"

Smooth as silk Glixen followed the change in topic. "They are proceeding extremely well. The DNA design I used for the zygotes will be well within the top five percentiles of the gharian ideal for males".

"So, there are no females in the whole group?" Jax queried as he settled back in his chair.

"I could have used a proper ratio of male to female, but you commanded that I rewrite the DNA as little as possible. The base DNA material used was from two males, hence the hatchlings will all be male".

It made sense, and it would make dealing with an influx of two hundred gharians easier in the long run. Interaction with the gharian species had always been with the males since females stayed on the planet of their birth for their entire lifetime. If Jax were to be entirely honest with himself, the child producing males did also. Running around the universe as mercenaries and explorers was the work of casteless males that had no attachments to a family. The introduction of females to the

86

gharians aboard the stolen ships could change the dynamic of gharian interaction in ways that wouldn't necessarily be for the better. Shrugging his shoulders over things he didn't have to worry about right this moment, Jax thought of a question. "So, if you aren't rewriting the DNA, how can you be sure the hatchlings will be close to the gharian ideal?"

"Perhaps I misspoke. I did not write any more code than I had too. After speaking with Ja'Zarha, I found the desire for strong, athletic hatchlings with a keen intellect and instinct sense. Since the hatchlings design settled after the promises you made them, writing the gharian code required I ensure each zygote had the genetic predisposition for the desired traits. Basically, I wrote the DNA sequences to match the anticipated traits. I had to fulfil the bargain you made captain".

Jax spluttered the hot root tea he had been sipping. "Wait a minute. I never made any agreement! You are the one that made that promise Glixen. I just didn't see any way around it after the incident with your scat!"

"You could look at it that way. Or you could chalk it up to *(No Translation)*"

Jax used a cloth to wipe the liquid from his shirt as he replied. "Glixen, you are going to have to add whatever it is you are talking about to your translation software. Get Hed to help you if you need it. I think I better know exactly what the translator isn't saying".

"As you command captain. Do you have anything else for me?"

As you command? When did Glixen ever talk like that? Jax's unease over the whole situation graduated into sincere trepidation.

"Just how many hatchlings did you develop Glixen?"

"Ja'Zarha requested two for each crewman and four for each officer, but that created friction amongst the gharian crew".

"Okay, so what did you decide on?" Jax realized that being in the center of a confrontation amongst the gharians would have been terrifying for the cthichek.

A Pirates Booty

"I did what was needed for the continued harmony of your crew".

Jax purposely clasped is hands in his lap forcing himself to calm. "How many Glixen?"

The turret of Glixen's vehicle began to sway back and forth. The cthichek must really be getting emotional. "Five for each gharian serving now with an understanding that three will be made available for gharians that join us in the future. All the gharians demanded that the original members of the freedom clan have preferred status".

Jax tried to recall just how many gharians they had across all three ships and failed. "Just how many is that?

"With the added gharians freed from Podunk and the losses

we received fighting the SITC destroyers, there are a total of 51 gharians across the three ships". Glixen hesitated before continuing, as if deciding whether Jax could perform the basic math equation in his head. Apparently *ne* decided it wouldn't hurt to do the math for him. "That would be two hundred fifty-five hatchlings captain".

Three hundred and one gharians running around free. Jax had to wonder if they would survive the experience. At least he had some time to prepare for the event. Perhaps it wouldn't be so bad, they could build a gharian nursery when they found a planet to settle on and Jax probably would never even deal

with the hatchlings directly.
Fidgeting with his mug, Jax
responded. "How long do we
have until the hatchlings…
hatch?"

"They will begin the process
by the end of next week. By the
middle of the week after they
should all have hatched".

A quick estimate put them at
the location Glixen had given him
in about three months. Should
there be no suitable planets there,
they could be searching for
several months just for a place to
settle. That meant months with
baby gharians running all over
the ships. Ships that had every
spare space filled with power
crystals. Damn.

There was no way around it.

"All right, we better tell
Maddie to print out two more

crates. One for crystal storage and one to use as a nursery for the gharians. How many gharians will need to staff the nursery Glixen? Do you know?"

"Gharian do not use others to care for their young, captain. Males care for their own young. Upon hatching, the progeny attaches itself to the males hide to live in a symbiotic relationship until grown enough to fend for themselves. Rather like the remora that attach themselves to sharks and other marine species on human terraformed worlds".

Jax had a headache. "I see. Well tell Maddie, Captain O'Kleif, to print out another cargo crate and another personnel crate anyway. It looks

A Pirates Booty

like we will be needing the space
regardless".

Chapter 6 – Unnatural

*Drake – The Gold Digger –
Between the Milky Way Galaxy and
Andromeda*

$\mathcal{D}$rake could appreciate beauty. He had an art appreciation sub routine built into his basic cybernetic suite. This was different. As he watched Baylee towel off in the steamy cabin, he understood that her lithe form and regular features fit the profile of humanistic beauty. Men drooled and acted like fools around her, a sure testament to the effect she had on the male species, and some of the females as well.

A Pirates Booty

Drake had worked with Hed and Glixen to made sure his cybernetic reproductive systems acted and functioned perfectly. A small addition to his knowledge chip made sure he used them properly and to affect a desired response from Baylee's sexual response systems.

To put it mildly, the sex was good, really good. Then again, anyone with a data slot could purchase knowledge programs for sexual and sensual prowess for less than three credits. Should she choose any of the crew would be happy to be with her.

So why was she here with him?

Drake turned to one side. He could feel the beginnings of another malfunction of his reproductive organ as Baylee

strode nude across the room. He
would have to talk to Hed about
getting the software checked. His
reproductive system randomly
prepared for sexual congress at
inappropriate times. He grabbed
the book he had been reading and
placed firmly, if painfully, over
his lap. He refused to be
humiliation from his
malfunctioning system in front of
Baylee.

If he hadn't lost so much in
the enhancement process perhaps
he would understand better.
When Arrex Ten had tried its
new cybernetic creation process
for the first time on Drake it had
tossed away areas it felt were
non-essential. Thing like
memories and emotions. Hed had
done a wonderful job putting

things back together, but you couldn't replace what you didn't have. Drake remained broken and he knew it. Dedication to Jax and feelings for his sister Baylee kept Drake going. The 'fake it til you make it' had become his daily mantra.

Eventually he hoped to be normal again but he feared the mental and physical damage he had received from Arrex Ten made the hope a vanishing dream. He was like the character in the classic book he was reading. A being created for purposes not his own to accomplish deeds not of his choosing.

Frankenstein had nothing on Drake.

Insane engineers created both Drake and Frankenstein's

98

monster without caring for the thing they created. Neither Drake nor Frankenstein's monster remained human.

Drake existed as Arrex's monster.

Baylee could never know the abomination that Drake had become. None of his friends could know. He could not bear the look of horror they would give him. If they knew the hollowness he felt inside, they would spurn him as the monster he had become.

Baylee dressed slowly holding up clothes and tossing them aside. The peek a boo effect disconcerted Drake to no end. The discomfort from his maladjusted sexual organ became pronounced as he squirmed on the edge of the bed they shared. Drake pressed the book hard against his groin hoping to quash the sensations. It didn't do any good.

Drake had to use the happy expression subroutine to smile back at Baylee when she winked at him.

Like Drake himself, the smile felt unnatural. Baylee didn't notice, no one ever did.

Chapter 7 – Git Along

Lil' Aliens

Jax – The Jack Ketch – Between the Milky Way Galaxy and Andromeda

Six weeks of endless black space. Six weeks since the conversation with Glixen about the gharian hatchlings and the decision to go to the Tortuga system. Preliminary reports showed navigation into the area Glixen had marked would be every bit as complicated as Jax had feared and then some. Besides the gravity wells caused by the twin suns and the nearby black hole, there were nebulae that floated about the area that emitted all manner of energy that promised to play havoc with the sensors. Captain Maddie had flatly refused the destination until Glixen and Hed had sent her the navigational path they would take. Even then she had to be given assurances that the predefined path would be safe. Luckily Captain Drake didn't care where they went, and the possible dangers didn't faze him one single bit.

Glixen and Hed had been acting strangely though. Glixen ever since the non-translatable declaration in his office. Hed claimed he was working on a translation, but of late he seemed to be avoiding queries on his progress. Jax had also noted that

Hed and Glixen spent a lot of time together. Since Hed was the only promach on the three ships, just like Glixen was one of only two cthichek, Jax had to assume they shared an outsider view and preferred spending their off time together.

The hatchling gharians were not the problem Jax had foreseen initially though. They did just as Glixen had stated and attached themselves about their fathers hide, dangling about their parent like living jewelry. They were kind of cute even. Jax had learned the hard way that they responded to the touch of others as they would a free meal though. When he had tried to pet one (he would never admit he had made baby cooing noises to the tiny lizard) the hatchling had taken a chunk out of his finger. Ja'Zarha had simply pulled the wayward lizardling off Jax's skin and slapped his back explaining he had to spit it out, it was nasty and would make him sick.

Jax managed to have his fingertip regrown at Dr. Claudeburge's office and settled for a look but don't touch policy when dealing with the gharian young.

Jax was going over the reports from the *Gold Digger* and the *Kraken* when Ja'Zarha and Hed chimed for entry. The head of the gharian troops wore a bright purple silk shirt with black leather pants and an array of gold jewelry that included a golden net wrapped over his tail. Twin

bandoliers across his chest
containing recharge batteries for
the pistol on his right hip along
with the sword and countless
knives about his person lent an
adding air of menace to his
countenance. Just the sword was
a marvel. Fitted for Ja'Zarha's
9'7" height and fifteen-hundred-
pound mass, the bar of sharpened
black hole steel could have split a
full-grown cow in two.

Beside him floated the golf
ball shaped environmental
vehicle Hed preferred. Hed's
environmental vehicle looked like
a child's playground ball beside
the towering gharian. The small
jellyfish looking creature that
resided within was anything but
innocuous though. Jax had seen
the small promach down a SITC

frigate by himself by hacking into their computer to take command of their control systems. Jax preferred these two solidly on his side.

Jax rose to greet them as the door opened. "Ja'Zarha! Hed! It is good to see you. How can I help you?" Jax watched two of Ja'Zarha's offspring climb to settle on the top of his head to watch the proceedings. Jax made a mental note not to allow them to distract him. The little things were just so damn cute the self-admonition would be easier said than done.

"Greeting captain." Ja'Zarha responded ignoring the mock battle now taking place on his head.

"Captain we want some franging wart answers". Since

gaining his freedom Hed had
adjusted his translator to respond
with much more colorful
language than had been available
to him when indentured to Arrex
Ten as a battle hacker. Jax
wondered if the translation
software added the color, or if it
now translated more accurately
the way Hed spoke. He supposed
it didn't matter.

Jax responded as he motioned
for Ja'Zarha to take a seat and for
Hed to settle his vehicle onto the
table. "I am happy to help. I will
answer any questions to the best
of my knowledge".

Hed took the lead. "I looked
at the leprous mange rat infested
system you are taking us to. Not
only will navigation be so
complicated as to challenge even

my superior mathematic skills to find a safe path through that quasar infested rot pit of space, but the planets there have such an erratic orbit who knows if any of them will be remotely usable for our purposes. There is no way we will be able to get any useful data on any of the planets in the system until we are in it. Once we are in there are no guarantees we can get out."

Jax waited a moment to be sure Hed had finished before answering. "We knew that when we first started toward the area, and did you say quasar?"

Hed responded as soon as Jax finished speaking. "Yes, I said energy storm, gravity sucking, quasar. You know, as in groups of black holes emitting all kinds of Thrace be damned energies.

There are parts of the navigation path we will have to take that will be a lot like taking fire from a lance of human prowlers. You may come from a backwoods dirt planet in a society that mixes animal feces with dirt to grow your food, but even you should know what a quasar is. Let me put it in terms even you can understand. Quasar hurt ships. Hurt ships empty creatures inside into space. Quasars kill creatures. Quasars bad. Open space star systems good".

Being talked down to by a member of a species that were about the size of his two fists together and had less surface tension of a drop of water didn't sit well with Jax. "Perhaps you should have made your complaints when I first told everyone where we were going instead of waiting until we were two thirds of the way there".

"Perhaps you should have told us everything you knew about the destination". Though the words came from Hed's translator without rancor, the snippy reply didn't need inflection to portray Hed's ire.

"I can't tell you what I don't know! You yourself said you just got this information".

Ja'Zarha spoke in his gravelly bass voice. At least the sound came from the gharian even if his translator adjusted the words to human common. "Then we will find another destination?"

Something about the way the two were double teaming him didn't sit well with Jax, causing

110

him to feel more stubborn than usual. This whole conversation felt as if they had rehearsed their part and expected the answers they received. Jax retorted as his hand unconsciously slid to the weapon on his hip "And where would that be? You both agreed to the destination. Are you saying you are afraid to travel there now? Perhaps we could find a nice planet we could share with the same people that made us slaves. I am sure they would coddle you and care for you and make sure you didn't have to do anything dangerous". Jax put more venom in the words than intended and he was sure the translators would relay that, but right now he didn't care.

A Pirates Booty

Ja'Zarha leaned in from his seated position. "So, you refuse to alter your decision?"

Jax couldn't help but watch as a third young gharian join the first two atop Ja'Zarha's huge head staring intently at Jax in an imitation of the patriarch's stern scowl, his tiny teeth shining in the light above the enamel blades of Ja'Zarha's fangs.

Jax refused to be intimidated on his own ship. "Unless you have a better reason, no. Besides, basing ourselves in the middle of that area keeps any outsiders from finding us. We have enemies. a lot of them. Anything that keeps them from finding us or coming in with guns blasting if they do find us, is ideal in my book".

Hed interjected his own comment. "You are saying that Glixen's request to go to this system has no bearing on your decision?" This double teaming was really starting to piss Jax off.

"No, I am not saying that. Glixen recommended it. Everyone agreed. We are going there. As I said before, if you do not have specific reasons, meaning you cannot navigate your way there through fear", Jax glanced meaningfully at both aliens, "or incompetence, our destination remains the same".

The chair creaked ominously as Ja'Zarha leaned back with surprise at Jax's harsh words. Looking over at Hed's spheroid vehicle he nodded knowingly.

"Very well, we understand. I trust you understand what we do also". Ja'Zarha stood as he spoke, the young gharians scrambling for a better spot before his head brushed the ceiling.

Jax jumped up alarmed. Ja'Zarha's words had implications of mutiny. Jax suddenly regretted his harsh reactions, but if this was where they were going, the rehearsed way they had double teamed him revealed that they would have mutinied anyway. This whole meeting was just an excuse.

Tearing out his own blade from its scabbard with his right hand and his pistol from its holster on his left, Jax set himself with his back to the corner of the room prepared for the worst.

With a slightly bowed head Ja'Zarha began to speak with Hed in a tone that sounded both ominous and formal. Jax held his place ready for anything.

"I would offer myself, my life and my freedom as assurance that I am loyal to you". The conjoined voices sound eerily familiar. Jax tried to remember where he had heard those words before.

Ja'Zarha continued alone. "Formally and without reservation I, Zhara of the Freedom clan of the patronym Ja derived from our founder Jax also known as Captain Jax, declare *(No translation)* upon the person of our champion Jax of the *Jack Ketch*. This formal declaration supersedes all others and denies the right to make new declaration without specificity from all parties. I, Zhara of the Freedom clan of the patronym Ja pronounce *(No translation)* y Captain Jax. May the union *(No Translation)"*.

It was the same statement Glixen had made before *ne* started acting all weird towards Jax. What the heck was going on? Before Jax could comment Hed began in a rolling voice. "Formally and without reservation I, Hed of the promach twelfth family declare *(No translation)* upon the person our surrogate Jax of the *Jack Ketch*. This formal declaration supersedes all others and denies the right to make new declaration without specificity from all parties. I, Hed of the twelfth family declare the rising of a thirteenth family bound in creation to Captain Jax *(No translation)* y Captain Jax. May the union *(No Translation)*".

"What in the world are you two doing?" Jax managed to answer, wondering if his entire alien crew had gone insane.

"We do what we must for the good of our people captain. You, more than any other, determine the fate of the newly formed freedom clan. Glixen has bound his caste upon your person and by *(No translation)* you are bound to care for the cthichek of your *(No Translation)*. I have decided the gharian require no less protections as well as we provide no less *(No Translation)*". Ja'Zarha looked earnestly to Jax with all

117

five of his hatchlings resting upon his shoulders as if in witness to the event. For some reason Jax wanted to reach up and pet the tiny reptiles reassuringly. He knew better though.

"I do so for much the same reason Jax, though the ability to create the thirteenth family draws strongly upon my heart. For thousands of years the promach have kept the twelve families in stasis in the belief that thirteen is the number of chaos. I choose to break the chains of myth and create the thirteenth family here in *(No Translation)*. So, don't get your panties in a twist captain. The thirteenth family will be fully bound by *(No Translation)* You can't be any worse than scat breath Arrex, we won't let you".

The bowling ball size, golf ball looking environmental vehicle Hed used seemed to glow with energy.

"I do not accept!" Jax yelled. "I don't know what you are doing but I get to have a say in all this, don't I?"

The two responded in unison, "No."

Hed felt the need to add, "Jinx, you owe me an argon spritzer".

Ja'Zarha turned to glare at Hed. "Why would I give you an argon spritzer? You can obtain one for yourself at the food printer".

Hed levitated his vehicle a foot over the table. "Those are the rules of *(No Translation)*. Here, I

will send you a copy, lizard
brain, if you don't believe me".

Jax had had enough of all this
nonsense. "The term is 'jinx, you
owe me a soda pop' but that is
just an old expression when
people say something at the same
time unexpectedly. It is not a law
or anything".

Hed sounded triumphant.
"Yes, but you're human, well
cyborg anyway, and a 'soda pop'
would be dangerous for my
health. A soda pop a vile
concoction that's better used to
cool a witch's teat, in my opinion.
I took the liberty of translating
the expression to a consumable
liquid more appropriate to my
species. Unless your
unimaginative brain cannot
accept such translations, then I
will of course consume the

120

visceral sludge brought to me by Ja'Zarha under *(No translation)*".

Jax was becoming flustered. "How in the world do you expect me to follow rules I can't possibly understand because they are literally not translatable? This just needs to stop".

"Too late". Ja'Zarha and Hed replied together. This time it was Ja'Zarha who responded first.

"Jinx. You owe me a Squirming Lianden Leech!" He seemed very pleased with himself for beating Hed in the game.

Hed had his own response. "Not if Captain Jax says we have to drink soda pop! You do realize soda pop is made from carbonic acid mixed with a bunch of $C_{12}H_{22}O_{11}$ to ensure torment when ingested don't you?"

A Pirates Booty

"Captain Jax would not force us to consume such garbage! We are under *(No Translation)* He is responsible for our wellbeing". Ja'Zarha looked horrified at the idea of being forced to drink soda pop.

Hed reminded the gharian of the full agreement. "Yes, but we are also bound to act upon his dictates up to and including foul standards of internal self-mutilation from the customs of his birthplace. We can only ask how to interpret such matter from Jax himself".

"Drink whatever you want. Why would I make you drink something that would harm you? You are going to have to explain what it is you are doing in terms that can be translated". It must be the weeks and weeks of being in the darkness of space in between galaxies that had his crew acting so strangely, like cabin fever.

"We will find a way to explain it to you under *(No Translation)*". Ja'Zarha promised. "For now, we will return to our duties".

Hed had to add his own comment, "I will tell Captain Maddie we require another ton of organic material for the food printers as well as another ton of ore for the metal printers".

Jax had to ask. "Why do you need the resources Hed? You know we are trying to conserve since we don't know when we will be able to resupply".

Hed responded with all the aplomb a floating sphere could, "For the thirteenth family. You need to listen before you agree to anything Captain. If you are not careful you could agree to things you never knew about".

All Jax could do was face palm with one hand as the other shooed the two aliens out.

Chapter 8 – Keeping Up

*Baylee – The Gold Digger –
Between the Milky Way Galaxy and
Andromeda*

Baylee slid another stack of requisitions over to go through. Who would have ever thought a pirate fleet ran on paperwork? Pirates were supposed to be free and fun loving. A raid here and drunken party there, no one ever said anything about material requests or consumables or sleeping quarters for differing species. She refused to complain though. Anything was better than the dregs of a life she had lived on Podunk. Here, as Jax's sister, everyone respected her. They treated her with a deference she could never have received on Podunk. Should that not be enough, if anyone dared upset her Drake took care of it. The man could be fanatical about Baylee's wellbeing. She felt warm inside with the idea. After a life spent fighting for survival having someone care for her was a new experience. An experience she could easily grow accustomed to.

Drake was perfect. He was everything she wanted without even knowing she wanted it. Always a gentleman, except when he wasn't. At those times he became a dervish of strength and power. Watching him work out in the gym sent thrills down

126

her spine. He fought like the god of war and moved like a panther. Just the thought had her stomach turning with butterflies.

He was the best man she had ever met. She loved Jax, but her brother had too many issues from his captivity to really get close to. Jax had brought her Drake and freedom though. For that she owed him a debt she could never repay.

The inter ship comm came up on a personal line. Glancing at the readout Baylee saw Maddie was on the other end. Tapping the engage button she leaned back in her chair, rubbing the beginnings of a headache from the bridge of her nose.

"Hey Maddie! Whassup!"

A Pirates Booty

The screen showed Captain Maddie of the *Kraken* lighting up a stogie with panache. "Evenin' lassie. How goes the paper war? Everythin' workin' like we figured?"

Baylee leaned back forward as she spoke. "It looks like we will have just enough to get everybody what they want. Not a lot to spare though. Thanks for the inventory, Maddie. It came in handy figuring out what we could get away with. Now I just have to authorize the expenditures and we should be good to go."

Maddie nodded. Taking a huge puff of her cigar, she blew out a blue gray cloud of smoke as she spoke. "I told ye it'd all work out lassie. How go things wit yer boy toy? He still performin' as advertised?"

Baylee smiled. "Oh yeah. Maddie, I am so happy it kind of scares me. Scares me that this is an illusion that will evaporate at any moment. Drake is everything a girl could want."

Maddie chuckled. "I remember lass. Me and the mister were likenin' to peas in a pod when he was alive. He wasn't all fancy like your Captain Drake, but he was solid, and he was mine. Tell you true, the fancy ones always worried me a mite."

Baylee shoved the papers aside. She would deal with them another time. "Why is that Maddie? Too much of a good thing?"

A Pirates Booty

Maddie waved her cigar in the air as she spoke. "Naw. Truth be told, I'd not mind a bit o bedroom antics with Cap'n Drake meself. It's more like me eld mam used to say. 'Never latch a purty boy. You always has'ta compete for his love.' Not that I ever had a chance ta latch a purty one mind you."

Baylee stared at Maddie across the vid. Was she trying to tell Baylee something? "Should I be worried Maddie? Have you heard something?"

Maddie waved away the clouds of smoke that had begun to encompass the vid view. "Don't you worry nary a bit, lass. Just an expression. You an Cap'n Drake go fit a bread and jelly. Never you mind an old woman's rantings."

The conversation dwindled down for several more minutes before they made their farewells and disconnected. Maddie's comments wouldn't leave Baylee though. Was she destined to lose Drake? Would he tire of her when other women offered themselves up?

Baylee concluded it didn't really matter. Bayle had been with a lot of men and he had never once complained or even mentioned it. She would take the relationship for all she could. As long as Drake came home at night, she would have a warm bed for him to come home to.

It might not be a bad thing for her to up her game a bit though.

Chapter 9 – Forced Maneuvers

Captain Drake – The Gold Digger – Between the Milky Way Galaxy and Andromeda

Drake shattered the tumbler against the bulkhead. His mind spun as he watched the crimson liquid of his drink create runnels to the floor.

They asked for too much, but how could he refuse? Jax was his family. He loved Jax like a brother. Even more since Drake had never had a brother. What they intended felt like betrayal of the worst kind. Drake had told the others that they should go to Jax with the plan and let him decide rather than forcing Jax into an untenable position. He had been resoundingly outvoted.

He could see their reasoning. Jax remained dedicated to the concept of a free peoples. The problem with true freedom lay in the chaos of hundreds of individual choices, often at cross purposes. They simply could not afford to be unfocused. Every crewmember had to be fully in line with their purpose to get to where everyone could reap the benefit of freedom. Even then there would need to be those that stood vigilant to keep it.

A Pirates Booty

Drake could see their reasoning but that didn't mean he agreed with it.

He would rather battle the entire crew than betray the trust Jax had in him and he had said just that to the others.

Until Baylee had told him she wanted enhancements of her own.

The idea had so flabbergasted him that he could not respond as she explained her reasons.

She listed the ability to keep a copy of the records in her memory for faster processing and the ability to take care of herself in combat so she wouldn't be a liability. They sounded like excuses more than reasons.

But that wasn't what had upset Drake.

She wanted enhancements to be able to keep up with him. Enhancements that would give her strength, intelligence, stamina, and beauty. Enhancements designed so she could stand beside him when he performed duties only an enhanced could do.

Drake had been unable to hide the look of horror that came across his face before she saw it. He turned away, but he was certain she had seen it.

When she broke down crying, he jumped to console her. She sobbed about needing to keep up with the other enhanced onboard ship and she couldn't keep up with everything. In a voice hitching with tears she said she had to be able to do better, too many people depended on her.

Drake stood to get her a cup of hot tea as he told her she was doing great. If she found herself overwhelmed, they could find an assistant, or even two to help her.

Eventually she settled down and he lay her in her bed drawing thew covers over her. He promised he would be back after checking the *Gold Diggers* systems and his staff.

Just as the door was closing, he heard her. In a voice he would not have noticed had he normal human hearing she whispered. "Oh Drake. What will I do without you? You are going to hurt me. I know it." As he walked away stiffly erect he could hear her crying through the door.

She wanted enhancements to protect herself from him. Somewhere deep inside she knew him for what he was.

She wanted to become a monster to defend herself from a world of monsters. Drake ran diagnostics to assess the very real pain he felt in his heart. She feared he would hurt her. He could not imagine ever harming her but what monster truly intends the ill they spread. She asked to become a monster and he could not force himself to deny her.

That made him the most monstrous creature of all.

Chapter 10 – Yet Again?

Jax – The Jack Ketch – Between the Milky Way Galaxy and Andromeda

Before everything became said and done, four more crates rolled from the printers and attached to the lengthening train behind the *Kraken*. Maddie had printed a nursery and a play area for the young gharians. Hed had demanded two crates built to his specifications for who knew what reason which Maddie also printed. Another organic printer

138

and another metal printer printed
to be placed within one of the
crates as had a goodly portion of
their organic and ore supplies.
The entire process had slowed the
starships down considerably
while the crates rolled out and
were set in space. Everyone
involved in traversing between
the ships felt more comfortable
doing so at lower accelerations.
Even travel between two willing
starships could be extremely
dangerous at super light speeds.

Another factor of the building
became their dwindling stockpile
of ore and organic material.
When they had left the Milky
Way, Jax had expected to arrive
in Andromeda with enough raw
material to survive for a year at
least while they searched for new

sources. At the rate they were going they would barely make a month. It would take a month to start mining ore and growing hydroponics even if they settled on the first rock they found floating around on its own.

Captain Drake had been questioning Jax's orders since Ja'Zarha and Hed had taken supplies for their projects. Wondering aloud in Jax's presence why the aliens suddenly had such a right to the stores. Added to that Allie had been hanging around Hed and Ja'Zarha way too much for Jax's tastes also.

Jax would be ecstatic when they finally settled on a planet and had room to stretch out. This cabin fever that afflicted the entire crew always seemed to dump the garbage right into his lap.

Right now, he had a luncheon meeting with Captain Drake and his own first officer Allie. Jax only hoped they could straighten out what was going on with the crews. If things continued the way they were going, the entire group would starve and self-destruct in the cold black between galaxies before they ever saw planeside.

Right to the second, Allie and Drake entered the conference room together. As Jax smiled his best smile and moved to greet them, Drake dove right into the conversation.

"It is the will of the enhanced beings of the crews of the Freedom fleet that I come to

141

negotiate terms of service". Drake showed not an iota of emotion as he spoke the words.

"Oh, come on Drake, we have known each other for what, fifteen years or so? Since when do we have to be so formal? Allie, tell the big guy to relax and we can have a drink while we figure a way around this". Jax appealed to Allie hoping for an ally in what was starting to sound like a hostile negotiation.

"Jax, I am also of the enhanced beings Drake speaks of. All of us have decided to abide by whatever decisions are made here today". Allie's voice could barely croak recognizably as she followed some internal predefined path. Jax felt like he didn't know either of his closest friends as well as thought he did.

"C'mon you two". Jax couldn't get the pleading note out of his voice. "I have had to put up with this from the others, but I never expected this kind of treatment from you. There are only three enhanced beings in this whole fleet, and they are sitting right in this room".

Drake refused to sit or even show emotion, speaking as if from a script. "At present time there are two hundred fifty enhanced beings on the three starships *Jack Ketch*, *Kraken*, and *Gold Digger*. By the end of the week we expect all the human crew to have become enhanced in one form or another".

Jax felt himself sitting down without consciously willing himself to. Why in the world would everyone go through the pain and suffering becoming enhanced entailed? He couldn't fathom the concept. Jax had no idea how everyone was becoming enhanced in the first place. Before he thought about it any more deeply, he put voice to the words.

"Why would they do that? More importantly, how are they doing that?"

Drake answered as if expecting the question. "Dr. Claudeburge, Dr. Savage and Dr. Swango are performing the surgeries using software that Hed wrote and enhancements Glixen and Cooter developed. Each crew member chooses the enhancements they can afford given their credit in the purser's office".

144

Jax shook his head as he ran his hand over his scalp. "Baylee knows about this?" Jax's sister Baylee happened to be his only known living relative as well as the purser for their endeavor.

The answer came from Allie. "Yes. She herself will be having her enhancements installed by the end of the week".

His baby sister a cyborg. Jax had to stop this madness. Before he could go to confront Baylee about this nonsense another thought came to him. "Where are the materials for all of these enhancements coming from? We are low as it is. Raw material for all those enhancements would wipe out our stores."

Drake responded. "Baylee calculated we will have enough

organic matter for food and enough ore for maintenance functions for the three starships for two months with just a bit of rationing. By all calculations that should be more than enough to reach our destination".

Jax exploded. "And what happens when we get there? Even assuming there will be suitable planets with actual dirt instead of methane oceans or a huge glob of gaseous clouds, terraforming enough area for hydroponics and setting up mining will take months before we have any kind of return in raw material. If what you are telling me is true, we wouldn't last if we were going to land planet side tomorrow!"

Allie responded before Drake could. "Glixen has an idea for

146

that. I must tell you though, that the ramifications of the crew spending their share of the plunder before landfall will be for you to decide at another time. Currently, we wish to discuss another matter."

"We are going to starve to death in space in starships that won't fly because we don't have the resources to fly them because everyone decided to squander what resources we have on frivolity and you have more important things to talk about? Oh, please enlighten me". Jax could feel his heart pounding and his blood racing with the anger he knew he had to hold down before a fight ensued. A fight he would lose against his formidable friends. Overriding his anger

147

betrayal reared its ugly head. The two people he should be able to trust above all others had allowed, possibly even instigated, this madness without even consulting with him.

With a tortured look at Allie, Drake spoke in a monotone.

"Formally and without reservation I, Captain Drake representative of the enhanced humans aboard the three free starships of the freed indents in willing and full knowledge of consequence declare soul fealty of mind, body, emotions, desires, and dreams y Captain Jax upon the person of our liberator Captain Jax of the *Jack Ketch*. This formal declaration supersedes all others and denies the right to make new declaration without specificity from all parties. I,

148

Captain Drake of the *Gold Digger*, in keeping with the tenants and unanimous demands of all enhanced of the three starships *Jack Ketch*, *Kraken*, and the *Gold Digger* forever known henceforth as Captain Drake Jaxson claim soul fealty of mind, body, emotions, desires, and dreams y Captain Jax. May the union forever stand upon the strength of soul fealty and the recompense already received from this binding oath".

Jax stood without speaking for a moment after Drakes declaration. Finally, the words burst forth. "What in the world do you think you are doing? Do you think this is a joke? What, you heard Glixen, Hed, and Ja'Zarha say the same mumble

149

jumbo so you decided to put your own spin on it to make a fool of me? There is no 'soul fealty'. You made that up to cover the part of this nonsense that couldn't translate and beyond that I don't accept! I think we are done here. Come back when you have forgotten about this nonsense".

Allie interceded before Jax tried to physically throw Drake out of the conference room. "Soul fealty is a rare though accepted practice in all known species. The concept came from the cthichek and the Milky Way governments and corporations latched onto it like a leech. They soon tired of it when they found that soul fealty required freedom to enact. The grantor required liberty to enslave themselves like that. The reason there was no translation comes from the first treaty's that demanded certain parts be spoken in the grantor's native language".

Jax gulped down the glass of 120 proof alcohol to sooth his jangled nerves. "All of that is well and good, but I did not accept any of the so called 'soul fealty'. We just became free! Why throw that away for some alien concept that doesn't even come from our species?"

Drake mumbled something under his breath, too low for even Jax's enhanced hearing.

"Speak up Drake, might as well have everything out on the table!" Jax felt like he had never known the two strangers standing before him.

A Pirates Booty

"I said we don't know how to be free! Everyone on these starships has been an indent for their entire adult lives!

Right now, they are running around following any thought or emotion that strikes them. They have freedom without discipline, and they don't know or don't want to deal with it.

Don't you see? Freedom scares them. We need for you to enforce the discipline needed to give freedom a chance for everyone. At least until we can learn how to be free ourselves anyway. Freedom has responsibilities. Responsibilities none of us understand yet."

"I don't know the ramifications of this soul fealty stuff, but don't you see the ridiculousness of giving away your freedom to learn how to be free?"

Allie interjected. "Yes, a certain irony exists here, but you are bound as tightly as we are. The soul fealty of the cthichek means you are responsible for everything in the vassals' existence. We do not give the gift of our lives lightly; we give it trusting you will ensure our continued success. No one has ever escaped synth lord ownership Jax. No one in the history of human space travel. You did what no being has ever done and to be honest the repercussions of what had happened scares everyone silly. They need to know you are taking care of them through the bond they offer".

A Pirates Booty

Jax blustered, "But I would have done it anyway! I never asked for such dominion and I don't accept it".

Drake interceded, "Really? I ask for use of some resources and you deny me? Glixen claims soul fealty and suddenly he has all the resources he could desire, and you are defending his choice of destinations even through the perilous gravity wells and energy storms we know lay in our path? Hed and Ja'Zarha claim soul fealty and now there are little gharians and promachs running all over their own crates built from the dwindling supply you keep complaining about? It has been obvious how you favor those that have made the oath!"

"But I didn't favor them, everyone has a right to… "Jax

trailed off as he thought over what had happened. He had to admit it looked like he had been favoring anyone that had made the oath. He had been an easy mark because he remained flustered by what had been going on.

"Whether you meant to or not, the perception remains that you were. Decisions are made upon perceptions".

"But Drake, you and Allie know better, don't you?"

"We have to follow what we see as our best chance for survival. At least this way we got some of the things we wanted".

"So, what have you and Allie sold your soul for?" Jax was ashamed to admit that he had been the unthinking friend in the group.

Drake turned away as if he could no longer look Jax in the eye. When he spoke, his words came out measured and tightly controlled. "We both need some specialized psychological programs to be able to overcome the trauma and damage the control software left in our minds. Our minds require healing the lingering effects and mental scars from the experience. We each also asked for one other boon. For myself I desired the permanent captaincy of the Gold Digger. According to the ramifications of the soul fealty, you can do anything you desire with, or even to me. You can never take away my starship".

Jax shook his head in disbelief. "You already had the Gold Digger. Why would I ever take her away? Even if I could that is".

Drake turned back to Jax his arms outstretched, all pretense of formality gone. "Regardless, that is what I made a condition for fealty".

Turning to Allie, Jax decided he better know all he could of this. "I am almost afraid to ask, but what is your stipulation Allie?"

Allie stepped up close to Jax their bodies almost touching, he could smell her clean scent as she looked him directly in the eyes with a clear challenge. "I am now officially the captain's girlfriend… sweetie cakes".

A Pirates Booty

Jax's hand fumbled over the comm button before activating it. "Baylee, I want you in the captain's berth right now!"

Chapter 11 – What It Boils Down To

Jax – The Jack Ketch – Between the Milky Way Galaxy and Andromeda

Baylee had made it to Jax's room before Jax himself had made his way to his quarters. Opening the hatch, he stepped through marching straight to his desk. Reaching into the bottom drawer he pulled out a crystal decanter and a tumbler showing the marks of consistent use and infrequent washing. After pouring a healthy dollop and downing it, he immediately

159

refilled the glass and took a smaller sip as his sister stood watching from the other side of his desk.

"Whassup big bro? Rough day on the bridge? All that telling everyone what to do wearing you down?" Her forced casual attitude didn't completely cover the worried creases decorating her brow.

"Can it Baybay. I want to know why you let me get blindsided by all this soul fealty nonsense. I want to know why you have been letting everyone spend our resources willy nilly for whatever project they thought was important, and I want to know when you intended to tell me you were going to get enhancements done". Try as he might, Jax couldn't keep the tang of betrayal from his voice.

Baylee used a few moments to get a glass and pour her own drink to gather her thoughts before resettling into the chair facing Jax. With a deep breath she responded, choosing her words carefully.

"Look Jaxie, it had to be done. When I was looking over the agreement that you had originally made with the crew before I came on board the numbers just didn't work. The captain's portion was only 8 shares, yet you take care of all the new projects. Any time a group became dissatisfied you had an emergency on your hands trying to keep everyone happy. You needed a power base, and you were too busy trying to coddle everyone to see it. Now you have it".

Jax settled his drink carefully on the desk. "Okay, I have a power base. That power base is not going to do any good when we starve to death before we can reload out food stores. Food printers need organic raw materials to print anything. A food printer might be able to adjust the molecular structure to imitate almost any complex molecule and link them in any combination programmed into the printer, but there needs to be base organic material to start with. There are strict requirements on the type of organic material printers use also. You know this Baybay. We both grew up on farms that grew the grain used in food printers".

"Yes, and I probably overextended the allotment required for enhancement. I swear I didn't realize just how much organic material went into enhancement surgery".

"And the ores for the metal printers? We are about out of that. We won't be able to repair ourselves either, which means that even if we find a way to feed ourselves, without a source of the raw ore we require for those printers we won't be able to search for a place to get it".

"You are being a drama queen Jaxie. There is enough raw organics to feed us for at least six months and once Drake completed his repairs from the last battle, we shouldn't need much maintenance. So, we miss a few oil changes. It will be okay Jaxie. You are worrying way too much".

Jax sat quietly for a moment before replying. He knew he didn't really know his sister very well since she had grown up on Podunk while he had been an indentured servant, or indent, for over fifteen years. He took a deep breath as he realized she had never had to deal with anything like being purser before he had come along. In fact, the biggest reason she had the job was that Jax trusted her and she had a lot more understanding of life outside the confines of an indent than he did.

But that didn't mean she knew everything or that she

always made good decisions. Jax tried to keep a moderate tone as he explained.

"The gharian hatchlings will be separating from their parent soon, that is why Ja'Zarha asked for the nursery crate. Growing gharians eat as much as a full grown gharian in combat because they grow so quickly. They require a lot of sustenance. That means we will have to feed over three hundred gharians soon.

Hed already moved the raw organic material you authorized for him to take to the two crates he asked for. We may have to put a hold on whatever project he started in there and save whatever material we can. We may even be able to break down the crates so we can reuse the metal".

Baylee winced as Jax explained. Her expression made it obvious she hadn't thought through the minutiae of her disbursement of their finite resources.

"We can't do that". Baylee almost whispered.

"Yes, Hed will be upset. But we can give him an even larger share once we have a way to replace the resources. He has done a lot for us. He is the one that broke Drake and Allie free of the control software to even give us a chance at escape. Even after we escaped, he hacked into that freighter over Podunk allowing us to get away with barely a shot fired. I admit we owe him, but right now we just can't afford the resources. Baybay I know you mean well, but you must tell me when you are doing these things. I will try to do this in a way that doesn't undermine your authority, but I am going to have to do it".

"But the crates are already made! We don't need the ore if we are careful!"

"The place we are going requires that we travel through several gravity wells and energy clouds. All the ships will take damage. We will likely have to perform some major repairs before we get to our destination".

"Then why are we going there? We don't have to go there you know. Hed has done a lot for us, more than you know what with the enhancements and

167

repairing the software for Drake and Allie and all".

"There are a lot of reasons for trying that particular place, but the fact of the matter is that we decided on our destination months ago. You had plenty of time to bring any qualms about it to me. Hed will understand, he may be a semi-gaseous life form the size of a grapefruit, but don't underestimate his intelligence. He is probably one of the best hackers in the universe".

"You don't understand. We can't take away the resources he took".

"Come on Baybay. We don't have a choice".

"No, you don't understand Jaxie. Think of the sheer programming and software repair Hed has done since we

168

started toward Andromeda. He rebuilt the software package for the *Gold Digger* from scratch. He just last week finished the combat software for the Kraken all while learning the most sophisticated combat software in existence here on the *Jack Ketch*. As a side note he developed trustworthy enhancement controls for the crew, and designed a package that would act as a psychological healing program for the mental damage done to Captain Drake and First Mate Allie. Damage they received from the control package Arrex put in. There are only a handful of hackers in the galaxy that would even understand how to approach problems like these, and he did it in the span of months, not the decades any software company would have taken. How do you think he did that Jaxie?"

Jax widened his eyes, taken aback by the revelation. "Well I assume that the other hackers helped him".

"Oh, you mean like that ex indent hacker Fleeke? He doesn't even understand half of what Hed is doing. In fact, he has just recovered from his own enhancement surgery. He added a data port and mathematical analysis suite as well as a complete coding index with the basic package just to be able to understand Hed's coding enough to be of some help".

"Okay. So how has Hed managed to get all of these things done?"

Baylee seemed to slump after the burst. Her eyes begged understanding when she finally answered in a rush. "He fissioned. In fact, by my best guess, he has fissioned eight or nine times since we started heading toward Andromeda".

"How in the world does that help?" Jax didn't want to admit he didn't know what fissioning meant in this context.

"Promach can breed by fission as well as sexual intercourse. They take on the organic material required, it takes more than you would think, and they split. Promach's are fully capable of reproducing asexually though there are societal as well as physical restrictions. When fissioning, both parts have the

171

knowledge of the parent. As they go on with life, they become separated by the differences in experience and environment the two new promach experience. Right now, there are just over two hundred fifty little Hed's working on software. We can't make them all their own environmental vehicles, so most of them do their work from their crate. He said he told you about the thirteenth family. This is how a new family is created".

Jax wondered how things had gotten so completely out of hand. "Okay so we can't recycle any of the resources used and I didn't figure in hundreds of promach when I estimated the supply requirements. That makes things even worse Baylee".

"I didn't know Jaxie, but I might have done all this anyway, given the circumstance".

"What circumstance? You have got to start telling me what is going on".

"You really are dense big bro. We have SITC madder than a wet feline because we defied their precious edict to be slaves. We have the dubious honor of killing a synth lord, which has never happened before I might add. Do you think they will sit back and be okay with that? The Milky Way governing accords hunt us as felons throughout the known universe. And with all of that, we were becoming splintered into factions. We had to be unified and you were the best option for

173

a focal point since you started all of this".

"This soul fealty thing makes everyone magically loyal? Somehow, I have trouble believing that".

"Believe or don't believe, what you think doesn't matter. What matters is that they all believe it. A lot of the crew wanted an excuse to ease the sudden burden of freedom they didn't know how to respond to. They also needed something to show that they weren't giving away their freedom without return so they are using species reproduction or enhancement as the coin of their loyalty. All of them know you will lead better than SITC or any synth lord. They also know the odds are stacked hard against us surviving another year".

"So, what am I selling my own freedom for Baybay?"

"Why, you sold your freedom for everything Jaxie. You personally own everything. The ships, the resources, even the crystals we harvested. We also reset the crew shares so that you, as the 'first captain', receive a hundred shares of any plunder gathered by the entire group. We figured this in as a sort of tax".

"You did all of this behind my back. Without even talking to me".

"Yep, sure did Jaxie". Jax realized his little sister looked rather proud of herself.

"You know I can't stand being called Jaxie, right?"

A Pirates Booty

"You know no one has called me Baybay since I was a kid, right?"

Chapter 12 - Monster

Drake – The Gold Digger –
Between the Milky Way Galaxy and
Andromeda

Stumbling into his cabin Drake grabbed a decanter of the strongest spirits he had and tipped the decanter to his lips. The liquid burned down his throat. The crew of the *Gold Digger* had designed the blend of alcohol and other intoxicants more for historical accuracy than for drinkability. Drake welcomed the burn. Anything to forget the look of betrayal in Jax's eyes.

Drake tried to tell himself it was necessary, but he knew he lied to himself as much as he had lied to Jax. Drake had gone along to get along, and in so doing proved he was the monster he knew himself to be. This was the price he would pay to keep Baylee safely at his side.

He marveled at how smoothly the lies had poured forth. Words that sounded good on the surface but even Drake didn't believe them. Jax had believed them though. Jax had believed the vitriol Drake and Allie spewed forth filling the air with any prevarication Drake could think of so Jax would go along. *What kind of friend did that?* Drake thought as he took another swig. *A monstrous one.* He answered himself.

Baylee interrupted his self-flagellation when the doors opened. Only Baylee or himself

178

could open the door to his cabin once locked.

When she entered her puffy red rimmed eyes showed she had been crying, hard. She ran into Drakes arms squeezing him so tightly he wondered for a moment if she had received her enhancement surgery in the past few hours without him knowing. Her tears soon wet the front of his shirt as her broken sobs muffled into his chest. Drake simply stood and held her, wishing he knew what to do to make her happy again.

When her sobs stopped Drake spoke in a gentle voice. "What happened Baybay?"

Drake waited for the time it took for her to get herself together enough to answer. "I

179

messed up Drake. I messed up bad. I didn't figure the right amount of materials we needed and now we could starve or be left adrift in space before we ever get to safety. He was so hurt Drakie. I have never seen him so sad. I hope we did the right thing. I couldn't bear the thought that we hurt him needlessly."

Drake lifted her one handed as he stroked her hair with the other hand. Carrying her across the cabin he hushed her. "We made the best choice we could given what we knew. You cannot be at fault for that. Jax will be okay, he just needs time."

Baylee nestled in the crook of his arm as spoke plaintively. "Do you really think so?"

Seeing her need Drake answered, "Of course." With that he laid her on the couch.

Baylee looked around the cabin smiling tentatively. "You just carried me across the cabin one handed without any effort Drakie. You really are a monster. Will I be able to do that when I am enhanced?"

Drake felt as if he had been plunged into the methane ocean of a frozen planet.

Chapter 13 – The

Frontier

Jax – The Jack Ketch – Sepia Cluster – Andromeda Galaxy

Andromeda. A harsh galaxy known for lawless boom planets, savage indigents, and freedom. Freedom from the tyranny of the Milky Way corporations and the corrupt government structures that supported them.

Three ill crewed starships, so unlike one another in design that had they been humans they would have been a motley crew indeed. Each reflected the persona of their captain by

182

chance more than choice; each as ready for a fight as a starveling dog living on junkyard scraps.

The *Gold Digger* and her new captain, Drake, sailed the stars majestically despite the ad hoc repairs scarring her hull. First launched from the military yards of the Starburst Interstellar Transport Corporation, the menacing lines and multiple gun ports marked this destroyer as a killer albeit an aged one. Launched under the name *Guardian XIII,* rechristened as the *Gold Digger,* the starship, like captain Drake, gave no false indications of polite intercourse. Each had been forged in battle to become killers of the most vicious sort.

A Pirates Booty

Maddie O'Kleif captained the *Kraken*. Both captain and starship had solid lines in an aging hull marked with a life of hard work and harder luck. Rechristened from *Grain Hauler 12*, the *Kraken* now sported military grade shields, more efficient FTL and in-space engines, a crew crate to allow in-space battle maneuvers, and a few nasty surprises for the unwary in the form of weapons deemed illegal for privately owned vessels in any star port where corporate governments existed. The work worn ship and her captain had broken free of the soul crushing regulations of her birth planet to find fortune in the new planets of Andromeda.

The third ship, the *Jack Ketch*, had sleek deadly lines and powerful engines to support

equipment and weaponry that
had no peer in the known
universe. Taken from the
laboratories of the synth lord
Arrex Ten, the new technologies
made this smallest of the three
the most dangerous. Jax, her
captain, as deadly in his way as
the Corvette class starship, led
the trio of mismatched starships
and the aggregate, multi-species
crew of over a thousand souls as
they decelerated into
Andromedin space. All three
captains sat before their
respective terminals focusing on
the next step in their desperate
bid for freedom.

On the bridge aboard the *Jack
Ketch*, Jax sat watching the sensor
inputs for anomalies. They had
been braking for weeks in

preparation for entering Andromedin space and the dangers therein. At super light speeds, even a grain of sand floating amongst the nothingness of deep space could spell out disaster if the sensors didn't see it or the clearing weapons missed destroying it.

Jax had decided to drop speed well below normal running velocities to account for the lack of solid maps for this area of space. Most of the data he worked with had come from projections based on sensor data procured on the fly that constantly updated itself as better data became available. Since the *Jack Ketch* had the best sensor array, she had taken point, closely followed by the *Gold Digger* with her banks of missiles and energy weapons. The *Kraken* rode drag, her shields and weaponry several grades below her sister starships, carefully trying to exactly match the path blazed before her.

The more data he received, the more worried Jax became. The quasar and the twin suns of the system that was their destination became more complex as the data flowed in. Even linking all three navigational computers for more computing power, the orbital paths and interactions between the celestial bodies remained a tangled mess. The first inklings of the types of energy storms they would have to cross became evident also. This was going to be one heck of a ride.

A Pirates Booty

Assuming they survived to be able ti ride it.

When the first energy storm came within five light years Jax ordered all shields at full. As the *Jack Ketch* slipped into the kaleidoscopic array of pulsating radiation, everyone sat on the edge of their seat in anticipation.

The effect was anticlimactic. Beyond the visual blindness and severely limited sensor return the hull didn't crash or vibrate, the power stayed solid. Everything seemed to be working better than expected.

So why did Jax still feel the cold knife of expectation pressing against his spine?

Communication between the ships crackled with the raging energy storm, but the ships were so close together it made up for the external interference.

Jax flipped the comm switch for reports. "*Gold Digger* and *Kraken* this is the *Jack Ketch.* Report status".

"*Gold Digger* at 100%" Drake responded promptly.

"Nothing but pretty lights as far as this old girl is concerned Jax" Captain Maddie O'Kleif responded.

"Excellent. Keep your shields at full and your sensors fully active. Comm me immediately if anything changes". Jax rubbed the sweat off his palms as he spoke.

"Affirmative". Came Captain Drake's answer.

"Yeah, you know it." Captain Maddie returned. "Don't worry

boyo. I'll let you know the moment anything comes up".

Jax was wondering if he had been overly worried about nothing when the first wave hit them.

Working the sensors, Allie called out first. "Energy spikes breaking into our shields a 43 percent total absorption captain. Still not enough to break through, but they are trying".

"How do the others look?" Jax responded crisply

"Both look good. The *Gold Digger* powered full shields and the *Kraken* has gone to full link shields on her cargo pods." Allie reported. The *Kraken* had a linked shield system to protect the towed crates, one of the reasons the *Kaken* required such a large drive and power system for such a slow starship.

"Reduce speed to match *Kraken*". Jax relayed to his bridge crew before pressing the comm. "Captain Drake, Captain Maddie updated status please".

"The *Gold Digger* is taking some superficial damage but nothing unexpected".

"So far so good for the *Kraken*".

Then things got hairy.

The course for the *Jack Ketch* spun on the navigation hologram. At super light speed, course changes were supposed to be gradual and careful. These changes came hard and fast. The g-forces from the quick changes were more than the gravity control system could completely control and Jax could feel the sudden pulls and twists of almost twenty g-forces in his bones as the *Jack Ketch* bounced around like a pop can in a dust devil.

Fighting the pull on his face and the pressures in his chest Jax yelled across the bridge. At least it felt like a yell, the sounds that came forth were more of a forced wheeze. "Hed, get us out of this thing!"

Amid the chaos, Hed's environmental vehicle stayed calm. The extreme protections the dimpled white sphere offered were necessary for the promach's survival. When he answered, his translator sounded calm and collected.

"I am trying but the Thrace be damned vectors are a complex array spun from that cosmic anal

192

quasar. I warned you this would be like riding an unpaid prostitute. I am countering as best I can, but the time it takes to send the command and for it to transfer to navigation and then retranslate after safety checks to the drives takes too long. The damnable galactic gravities we are encountering change more quickly than we can respond like this".

"Take direct control Hed. We can't go like this the whole way. Tell Hed on the other starships to do the same". Hed had yet to rename all the duplicates of Hed's fissioning, so Jax simply used the original name for all the promach.

Allie piped in with a barely noticeable strain in her voice.

A Pirates Booty

"Are you sure captain? That bypasses all the safety checks on the alterations. A missed decimal or incorrect sign and we would break us up so fast we wouldn't know it until after it happened".

Jax knew she was right, but the only reason he could even stay conscious lay in the enhancements that protected his heart and blood pressure. He also worried that the non-enhanced personnel could already be in a coma or dead. "I am sure Allie. Do it Hed".

For a few moments nothing changed, then Jax could feel the pressures lessening until it merely felt like he was commanding a starship from the front car of a roller coaster. Forcing his hand on the comm he hoped the other two ships were dealing with the gravity storm better than he had. "Drake, Maddie, you two okay?"

The sound of Hed's translator responded. "Captain Drake is unconscious from the extreme g-forces sustained with moderate injury. The Gharians are taking him to the med bay after he coated the surrounding area with the contents of his stomach in what I assume is a human defensive reaction. You humans are kind of gross. I received the required communication and am in direct control of the drives".

In the exact same translated voice Jax received an answer from the *Kraken*. "I have taken direct control as instructed and all systems are within tolerable parameters. The captain seems to have picked an extremely inopportune moment to explosively evacuate her bowels".

"Fascinating. You meat sacks are always surprising me with how you react to things". His own Hed added, the translators sounding like Hed talked to himself. "Perhaps the stomach contents have several orifices for ejection of food stuffs as a defense mechanism. I am going to have to research human and cyborg physiology. Perhaps 'spew monkey' would better describe your species".

Jax would have face palmed had he been able to move his arms freely. "Cut the chatter. Focus on the drives and getting us through this".

"Don't worry Sir Spews-a-lot, the 'retched' state we are in will be over when we squirt from the energy clouds into the Tortuga system." Jax couldn't be sure, but he believed that answer had come from the Hed on his own bridge. With the translators, all the promach sounded the same.

"Allie. How does our own crew look?" Jax squirmed in his seat as he tried to relieve the constant pressure of the gravity overpowering the systems.

"Dr. Claudeburge is having the conscious crew move the unconscious crew to the medical suites. He is drawing more power for the gravitic dampeners in that area". Allie responded, perfectly poised as if such little things as pesky gravity spikes had no effect on her.

A Pirates Booty

They needed as much power as they could get for maneuvering through this morass of bombarding radiation, power waves and gravity flux. Then again without any crew left the point became moot. "Tell him to take what he needs on my orders. Let Glixen know as well. Advise the other ships of what we are doing".

Allie turned in her chair to cast a curious glance back at Jax. "I already did. No need to order obvious actions I have already accomplished. Unless this is one of those male ego 'I am in charge' things. In that case then 'Yes SIR! Right away SIR! How would we ever survive, or even feed ourselves without your masterful guidance SIR!"

Someday… "Alright I get it Allie. No need to be sarcastic, we need to focus on the situation at hand". Jax tried to look as casual about the stresses on his body as Allie appeared, but wasn't sure he was quite pulling it off.

"Hed and Glixen have everything under control and I am keeping a monitor on all of our systems. I am merely catering to your male ego. I read that the male ego is an important factor of interaction between males and females. Such a small and fragile thing the male ego. I am surprised the species has survived this long. Speaking of small and fragile, the other day I saw you in the communal showers and I noticed…".

A Pirates Booty

"STOP! Just stop. I get it, sorry I gave you an order for something you were already doing". Jax had to wonder if all ship captains had this problem with their first mates having no respect. Never having hung around the officers of a space vessel, he didn't know for sure, but he didn't think most captains had this kind of problem. Of course, most captains didn't have a first mate that had decided they were the captain's girlfriend without input from the captain either.

The inter ship com crackled to life. The indicator said that the connection was with the engineering bay. "Captain Jax sir, I feel I need to tell you something". Glixen sounded hesitant. Of course, Glixen usually sounded hesitant.

I jolt of fear shot down Jax's spine as he mashed the response key. "What is it Glixen? Are the engines okay?"

"For now, yes. But there is a Cthichek here that wishes to advise a course change". For some reason Glixen recoiled from taking credit for anything. Jax sighed at the alien's roundabout way of speaking.

"Hed seems to have things in hand Glixen, I am not sure we should interfere right now". Jax scratched his chin. Since he had decided to grow a beard the itching came up at the most inopportune times. His hand felt like it was twenty pounds in the press of gravity from Hed's maneuvering of the ship.

"Yes, and Hed does a fine job. But I am not sure he knows about the vortex channel access point for the system. The other cthichek tells me if we miss the vortex tube we will be smashed to atomic dust. Just saying".

"Hed are you getting this?" Jax called across the bridge hoarsely as a surge in the g-force threatened to take his breath away.

"It's a Crenshaw infested base 65536 based vortex! No wonder I am having to make constant adjustments to this juking thrice be damned course. I was only using a base 16384! I am surprised we held together this long!" Hed's response didn't fill Jax with comfort.

202

"Can you do it Hed? Will it work?" Jax's face scrunched up as he powered himself to sit forward in his chair. The movement didn't help anything, in fact the strain on his muscles would leave him sore if they lived through this. Nevertheless, the movement made him feel better.

"I got it, but I don't have time for idle chit chat with an ignorant sasquatch. Glixen do you know the central vortices point?" Hed's environmental chamber seemed to float idly as he spewed his vitriol.

"It is not me! I said it was one of the other cthichek. I don't know why you insist…"

Jax couldn't stand it. "Glixen! Answer the question!"

A Pirates Booty

"Fine. Sending the spatial coordinates to base the mathematical development of the vortices now". Glixen sounded butt hurt. Jax decided he didn't care.

"What about the other ships Glixen? Will this plot work for them also?" Jax allowed the g-forces to slam him back into the chair. He had made as much of a physical statement as he cared to.

Hed responded before Glixen. "It falls to me to explain to the ignorant. The math Glixen sent to plot the ship requires the mass index of the ship, so your question has no answer as such. The formulae changes for each ship, but the concept is the same. I have sent my brethren the formulae, so the other ships are settling into the vortices channel

Glixen describes". As Hed spoke Jax could feel the g-forces crushing his body lessen. The effect felt like a bb fired into a funnel and rolling around the edge until it popped through the opening.

Taking the first full deep breath since they had entered the quasar field, Jax dropped his head. He couldn't help but wonder if Glixen had known the math required for entering the system all along. He vowed that he and the cthichek would have a long talk when things settled down.

Chapter 14 – New Vistas

Jax – The Jack Ketch – Peiratis cluster – Andromeda Galaxy

The rest of the trip through the quasar vortices became almost settled once Hed applied the correct mathematics to the plot. The optics showed a churning mass of bent light waves accented by flares made up of small bits of matter as they went nuclear from the stresses of the gravity bands.

The effect made for an impressive display if you didn't think about the star crushing forces battling a few miles from the circumference of the ships. Jax had to tell the crew to quit wasting sensor probes once they found out they could make an impressive display of nuclear holocaust when the sensors reached the sides of the gravity vortex.

Then he had to tell them to stop wasting furniture.

Jax lost his temper when he caught several crew members stuffing some hapless soul into the airlock. From what he gathered from the abashed crew, the person they were stuffing into the airlock for ejection had lost a bet about what color the explosion would be from ejecting a plate of gharian mollusks. After the incident Jake contacted Drake of the *Gold Digger* and Maddie of the *Kraken* to make sure their crews weren't about to do the same.

His warning came in time for the *Kraken* at least. Jax just had to retreat into his cabin when he saw money exchange hands when the explosion resulting from a *Gold Digger* crew member penetrating the vortex wall was rated and the specifics of the incident became known for the bookmakers to pay off.

They needed to find a place to settle as soon as possible. Jax shuddered to think of what his crew would find for distractions if they stayed in space another six months.

After a few days, even the prospect of firing different materials into the vortex wall lost its interest. Therefore, everyone was overjoyed when Hed let them know that they had reached the end of the vortex, and the planets of the multi-star solar system of Tortuga would soon appear. All three captains sighed with relief. The entire crew needed some place to blow off a little steam, even if they had to make their own port by blasting into the rock of a dead planet.

Jax happened to be in his chair on the bridge of the *Jack Ketch* when they were first hailed.

"Unidentified vessels. This is the Royal Cthichek Warden Vareyan, aboard the Empirical Vessel *Happy Thoughts*. Please state your names and purpose. Failure to do so will result in extremely aggressive action from our automated systems. I will not do this, so the consequences are not my fault."

Jax, stunned by the contact, took a moment to gather his thoughts. "Allie, get a bead on what we are facing and begin power up of the big guns. Make sure Drake and Maddie are powering up defenses and lined up behind us relative to the other ships." It took twelve minutes to power up the ship's antimatter dissolution emitters, but the weapon made for an awesome force equalizer. On the first test run for the weapon they had destroyed a respectable size moon.

Allie's response took less than a minute. "Looks like twenty stars ships of unknown design.

Displacement equals roughly that of the *Gold Digger*. More data as I can get it". Jax glanced over at his XO as she hunched over the screens, fingers flying over the sensor controls. Twenty star ships the size of the *Gold Digger* would swat them out of space like a gnat, even with their superior weapons and defenses. Assuming they had superior equipment. You just didn't go against that kind of tonnage with that kind of mobility with a corsair, a single destroyer, and a converted grain hauler.

Jax took a deep breath before responding, "This is the free ship *Jack Ketch*, escorting the free trader *Kraken* along with the free destroyer *Gold Digger*". Jax made sure not to mention the *Kraken's* battle modifications that made her a formidable war machine, or the fact that they had no trade goods to escort. Best to keep a few surprises.

"Be aware that the automated systems have a lock on your position and will open fire at the first sign of aggression. I do not choose this, as I said it is an automated system and it would not be my fault should you decide to self-destruct under our massive weaponry".

Allie updated Jax even as she fine-tuned the sensors on her display. "I am showing active lock an all three of our ships from their armada. Keep them talking Jax. We have six minutes until the big boys are ready to play".

"*Happy Thoughts* be advised we are a peaceful group of

traders looking for raw materials. Should violence occur, it would be your fault. Yours and yours alone". Jax spoke hoping the cthichek he was speaking with had the same personality issues his own engineer Glixen had. Namely an inability to take responsibility along with an abhorrence of confrontation.

"You state mistruths *Jack Ketch*. The systems automatically act which means I have no control of them, ergo it is not my fault. By engaging in falsehood, you have become an aggressor and the automated systems, not myself, will now engage. I am sorry that they will destroy you and your ships at this time. Please do not think ill of us since you have done this to yourselves". Jax had never been so passively attacked before.

The lines of energy and kinetic cannon fire were anything but passive. "All ships full power forward shields. Use all lower grade energy weapons to take out those kinetics. Allie will mark a single target to focus your heavy weapons upon. We will have to take them out one at a time". Jax released the com-link to call across the bridge to Allie. "Allie, how long until the big guns are ready?"

"Two minutes Jax".

Two minutes could be a minute too long. The sound of the entryway to the bridge sliding open distracted Jax enough for him to turn to see Glixen in his environmental vehicle, a tracked unit that looked suspiciously like an old earth tank, roll onto the bridge. The voice of Glixen's translator seemed to come from just over the turret.

"Captain, I would like to speak to the cthichek Vareyan. I have... information that may help".

As the first beams slammed into the shields, causing the entire ship to shudder and groan under the onslaught, Jax screamed through the chaos at Glixen. "Since you are not doing your job at engineering you may as well. Better be quick though, we won't be able to take much more of this!"

Jax stared at his screen as the lances of energy crashed into the *Kraken* and the *Gold Digger*. They were holding up, though not as

A Pirates Booty

well as the *Jack Ketch*. The few
return fire beams were damaging
a single destroyer on the other
side, but it would take too long to
cripple it. All three of his ships
would be space snot before they
even took out one of the enemy
destroyers.

"Did you hear me Glixen? If
you think you can settle this
better, do it now". Jax scrambled
to put on his battle suit when he
saw Allie moving away from the
console to get hers. Without it a
single breach of the hull would
end his life.

"I am speaking with Admiral
Vareyan now. I decided not to
use the audio system since that
form of communication is slow
and prone to misunderstandings.
A full translation is available on
your console". Had Jax not been

216

so preoccupied with the circumstances and getting into his battle armor in record time, he may have noticed Glixen's hesitation when answering.

Allie had her armor on and was at her console as Jax was still clamping on the under suit. She yelled across the bridge, "Weapons are up".

"Then fire the damned things! We are not going down without taking some of them with us!" Jax was stepping into his own powered armor as he yelled out the order.

The spacing of the enemy vessels didn't allow a firing line that would affect many of the ships. Allie opted for a full-on strike of one ship that allowed peripheral strikes on two other

217

vessels. Three ultraviolet beams appeared in space from the Antimatter Dissolution Emitters. Those beams simply disintegrated any known matter in their path for several light years. In moments one of the enemy ships had a perfect circle a meter-wide cut through the center of the hull and two others had holes along the outside hull.

At least they would know they were in a fight! Jax thought with savage satisfaction.

"*Jack Ketch*, this is *Happy Thoughts*. Please cease and desist, we surrender in the name of the emperor in absentia, Glixen, and by "*Non-Translatable*"give ourselves to the mercy of the great Captain Jax".

The onslaught ceased. Allie called across the bridge, "ADE

will be recharged for another salvo in one point three minutes. If we shut them down it will be another twelve minutes before we can fire them again. Your orders captain?"

Glixen's translator screeched. "No captain! On my life they are surrendering!"

Jax truly appreciated the Antimatter Dissolution Emitter, or ADE weapon system. But at times like these he truly hated the initial twelve-minute power up and the two-minute recharge times. Jax wasn't sure why they were surrendering but they had stopped shooting. From what he could see on the status reports rolling through his screen they had stopped firing just in time for the *Kraken*. The *Gold Digger* and the *Jack Ketch* may not have survived long enough for another shot from the ADE system either. Even if they did continue the engagement, the ADE could only take out a single destroyer at a time and while doing surface damage to two others.

Jax mashed the fleet comm button, "All ships stand down, but stay at battle stations."

Changing the comm to address the *Happy Thoughts* Jax growled, "We accept your surrender and whatever you called it." There really wasn't any choice.

Admiral Vareyan responded in flat tones. "Understood. Please travel to the coordinates I am sending now so that we may discuss terms and assign blame."

Spacefaring Buccaneer Series

Chapter 15 – Terms

*Jax – The Jack Ketch – Peiratis
cluster – Andromeda Galaxy*

The reports of damage were
still rolling in as Jax gathered
with Captain Maddie of the
Kraken and Captain Drake of the
Gold Digger in the armed shuttle
headed toward the rendezvous
point specified. Each captain
brought along a retinue of two
gharian marines fully armored
and carrying heavy quark
multiplier cannons. To ensure the
antagonists understood the multi-
species nature of his crew, Jax
brought Allie, Baylee, Glixen,
Ja'Zarha and the Hed from the

221

A Pirates Booty

Jack Ketch. He figured it didn't hurt having input from each species on the situation in any case.

All three of the free star ships had received major damage from the cthichek and his crews even now worked furiously on repairs. Jax still wasn't sure why the overwhelmingly more powerful force had surrendered to his small group, but he wasn't going to look a gift horse in the mouth, whatever the reasons.

Now Ja'Zarha spoke to the marine contingent in low tones. Jax assumed he was going over their guard duties as opposed to their normal search and destroy style work. Jax had grown so used to seeing the gharians with hatchlings crawling all over their skin, the lack of young seemed somehow out of place. Jax shook his head as he surprised himself at how quickly he had come to accept the little buggers.

Glixen and Hed pulsed to each other in conversation. The pulses and color of the light more aligned with the two species normal style of communication than modified sound waves. Watching them Jax wondered at the capabilities of the translators that allowed the communication between his race and theirs. Any understanding between their races remained only possible because of the translation algorithms designed to adjust their light speed communications to the cumbersome and often misconstrued sound wave manipulation humans and gharians used. Entire bank of data held conceptual information on file to allow for better understanding. He did know that many concepts did not easily exchange between species and worked with a "best guess" translation by the software. Some translations, like the strange allegiance they had offered him, flat didn't translate, and threw the software into a conniption. Jax still worried about the ramifications of that oddity while developing first time diplomatic relations.

As they passed into the shuttle bay of the alien vessel, Jax noticed the external hull of the ship had to be at least five feet thick. Marveling at the cost of such construction Jax couldn't help but stare through the portal looking for the seams that had to be there in what must surely be a double walled hull. Black hole steel remained one of the most expensive elements in the universe since it required molding to exacting specifications before compression and integration upon a star ship's hull.

Any repairs made on these hulls never matched the original hull integrity. The only feasible repairs overlaid a double thickness of patching material over the area and hot welded it in place. The patch was never as strong as the original but replacing an entire section of black hole steel took millions, if not billions of credits. Patches sold for a few hundred thousand.

A Pirates Booty

Few star ship owners could justify the extravagance of replacement.

The thought made Jax wince. They had just finished patching up the three ships a few weeks ago and now they had an entire new set of tears in the hulls. At this rate the hulls of their starships would shine with more patch material than standard hull material.

"Shuttle locking into the alien berth in 3… 2… 1… Now locked into place". Drakes informational relay brought Jax to the job at hand. Time to earn his pay, even if he didn't technically get paid.

"I want four marines through the hatch first. Report status as soon as you complete a full scan of the area outside the ship. Drake keep the engines idling.

Allie keep the weapons ready to fire. Baylee run a ship scan for anything we might have missed from the outside. Hed, see if you can infiltrate their computer system. Maddie see what you can do about personal shielding for us while we are inside this ship. We don't know why they fired on us in the first place so don't expect them to act in any way we could understand. On your toes people".

Each of his crew responded in the affirmative as the hatch clanked with the sound of the locks disengaging.

The environment the group entered had been set at just over a galactic standard gravity with an atmosphere so thick it almost felt like swimming. Without the

227

sealed battle armor the group would have choked to death before the poisons in the air could have killed them. Cthichek preferred living conditions meant an atmosphere filled with some caustic stuff.

Standing at the forefront with two gharian security personnel at each side, Jax ran a full powered scan from his battle armor as he waited for the cthichek representative. Running a passive scan while within the starship of another race could be considered the height of rudeness. Running a powered scan could be considered an act of war.

As the data began streaming into his feed, Jax reran the scan twice more to make sure of the information he was receiving. The cthichek starship he had

228

docked with used black hole steel
for interior walls as well as the
monstrously thick hull. The cost
alone had to be astronomical.
Before Jax could study the data, a
port opened in the far wall
disgorging several cthichek
crawling over each other like
crabs over a garbage pile.

With a full spread of five feet
claw tip to claw tip, the largest of
the delegation was about half the
diameter of Glixen, his own
engineer from the Jack Ketch,
while the others ranged in size
between fourteen inches diameter
and four feet diameter. The color
of their chitin ranged from a
mottled orange to a neon blue.
Looking at the crab like beings
Jax couldn't help but think that if

he only had some drawn garlic butter…

Jax jerked himself back to the reason he was here as his translator spoke in his ear. "I am General Raspit of the imperial defense force. I am here to offer *"No Translation"*.

Jax took a deep breath before answering. "Before I accept, I have to know a few things, such as why you attacked us in the first place".

Pinpricks of light shone from the largest cthichek as he responded. "We knew you traveled with Glixen. We did not wish to go to war, so we attacked you".

From behind him Jax heard Baylee respond incredulously. "You attacked us so you wouldn't have to go to war?"

230

Jax had to assume General Raspit was the cthichek that responded. "Exactly. I am glad you understand".

Jax held up his arm as he spoke. "No. We do not understand. You must realize the logic error in your statement. Explain your reasoning".

"Before Glixen was taken by the SITC raiders, he ordered us to fight to defend ourselves. The elder of the time commanded that we allow the few thousand cthichek the SITC corporation were taking to be abducted so that millions of others could live on in peace".

"They captured thousands of cthichek? And you did nothing to defend yourselves?"

A Pirates Booty

"Those taken had a chance of survival greater than the cthichek that would have fought. The elder of the time deemed this as good sense".

Jax shook his head incredulously. "And how did that work out for you?"

The light emitters on Raspit's carapace blinked furiously. "Unexpectedly, it didn't work out very well. After the SITC raid other corporations, as well as other races, began absconding our people by the thousands until the elders decided to hide within this cluster".

Jax didn't find that unexpected at all. "Wait a sec. Why would Glixen be able to order you into battle?"

"This was over four hundred years ago, so please take this in context. Glixen was only third in line to the emperor's seat at the time. Pellin graced the seat at that time. It was by his decree we allowed Glixen to be taken. Many at large cthichek say that Pellin died before his time of a broken heart from the loss of so many cthichek to raids. It was his successor, Cultat that decided we must find a place to hide from the raiders. Since that time few have bothered us here".

Jax began pacing as the cthichek situation clarified in his mind. "So that still begs the question. Why did you attack us?"

"After Glixen contacted us that he was free of Arrex Ten we knew he would return to impose his war. We could only hope to stop him before he stepped into the elder seat".

"Glixen contacted you?"

"Yes, from the very ship you arrived in. We have been building a defensive fleet since then, but we had no idea of the violence your ship would be capable of. We surrendered when our individual survival percentage dropped below 96 percent. No one in their right mind would battle against odds like that!"

Jax realized he was going to have to have a very, very long talk with Glixen after this. "Very well I accept your surrender. As a starting point I expect reparations for the damage done to our starships".

All the cthichek lowered themselves to scrape the deck

234

with their belly plates. "Of course, Captain Jax, though if I could make a suggestion?"

"Go ahead General Raspit".

"Rather than adding more patches to starships that are dangerously ill repaired, it would be better if we made new hulls for your ships of thicker material. The hulls you presently use allow an unacceptable chance of failure".

Jax tried to keep the excitement from his voice. "Well, if you think that is best. How are y'all set for organics and ore?".

Allie chimed in, "Some new assault armor would be nice."

Ja'Zhara had to throw in his list, "Our personal weaponry requires upgrade also."

Not to be outdone, Drake jumped in, "The Gold Digger and the Kraken will require engine replacements with more modern systems."

Jax smiled. If you were going to jump, may as well jump all the way. This so-called negotiation had to start somewhere. What he didn't expect was the answer General Raspit gave.

"Of course. I would like to point out that new armor and engines have an unacceptable chance of failure when attached to such an... archaic frame. May I recommend complete ship replacement? To your specifications of course."

The discussion turned into the oddest negotiation Jax had ever experienced. He soon learned why Drake had

236

christened his destroyer the *Gold Digger*. As purser, Baylee felt she had to exceed even Drakes most base tendencies toward avarice. Between the two of them Jax could only watch in awe.

Jax sat back and left them to it.

Chapter 16 – The

Cthichek Way

Jax – The Jack Ketch – Tortuga System – Peiratis cluster – Andromeda Galaxy

Once everything had settled, the cthichek fleet led the way into the planetary systems. Their circuitous route avoided many danger zones Jax would never have noticed or been able to avoid without a guide. If nothing else, this system promised security. Leaving Allie in command, Jax traversed the ship to the engineering bay to confront Glixen about his message to these cthichek. There were things going on with Glixen and the local cthichek Jax better know before they reached the cthichek stronghold.

When Jax entered the engineering bay he found Glixen working on the backup generators. "Glixen I think we need to talk about what General Raspit said".

If anything, Glixen seemed to become even more intent on his repairs. "I would not know what you are talking about captain".

Jax settled on top of a crate as he continued. "What about the whole, 'Glixen was third in line to the throne and he is now the elder of the cthichek' thing?"

"Yes, well that might matter if they had not allowed me to be

239

taken without any struggle. As it stands, I am under oath to yourself so I cannot serve on the tri council".

Things kept getting more and more complicated. "So, what is this council and what do they do?"

Glixen's appendages seemed to move even more determinedly as he responded. "Each population of cthichek has a tri council made up of the eldest member of each sex. The eldest male becomes Prime Minister and defining and interpreting how policy is to be carried out. The eldest female become Queen and enforces the law. The third of the triumvirate has always been the eldest *nemale* as the emperor. All policies and laws come from the emperor".

240

Jax whistled low. "Doesn't that make the emperor the most powerful cthichek in any population?"

Glixen paused in his work before answering. "Yes, so you see the curse of being born *nemale*. You do everything right and live a long life as you deserve only to find yourself with all that responsibility when you should be resting upon your laurels. The Prime Minister has entire legions of bureaucrats to carry out policy. The Queen commands armies of soldiers and legions of police officers to carry out law enforcement. Only the Emperor stands alone to take responsibility for everything. Of all the cthichek, The Emperor is most alone". Jax could feel the shudder underneath the words.

Gently Jax continued. "Just how old are you Glixen?"

After realizing *ne* had taken out and replaced the same rivet three times Glixen gave up on his task and focused on the conversation. "I was just past my second millennial when I was taken. Currently, I am just over two and a half millennials".

Jax kept the surprise out of his tone when he spoke. "How old is the next eldest?"

Glixen sighed. "*Ne* has not even reached *nir* second millennial. There is no way I can avoid the responsibility. My people will not let me. You can though. With my being oathbound to you, you must

242

accept responsibility. It's perfectly legal, I am sure of it".

The whole soul oath had started when Glixen had wanted to avoid responsibility. Several other things clicked into place. "So, what will your people do now?"

"Whatever you tell them to Captain. The entire population and their inhabitants have become your booty to use as you see fit".

"What about the Queen and the Prime Minister?"

"They are there to make sure your policies and laws are followed".

"Just to make sure I understand. You are saying that you believe I can go right in and start issuing commands with the

243

force of law and the army as well as local law enforcement will back me?" Jax couldn't hold back his incredulous tone.

"Yes, once the bureaucrats trace the proper agreements and historical precedents." Glixen seemed to be getting excited that Jax even entertained the idea of acceptance, or at least that Jax hadn't outright refused.

"And how long will I be expected to continue as acting Emperor?" Jax couldn't help but be fascinated with alien inner politics.

Glixen seemed to wilt a bit. "It is a lifetime appointment. Once accepted you cannot step down while still living".

"You are kidding right? I am going to just step in and take over the entire population of cthichek and hold power using cthichek law enforcement and military without even being a member of the cthichek species? This just doesn't seem right Glixen".

"I know, and I am deeply sorry your actions have put you in this position, but I am sure you understand that the agreement of *"non-translatable"* stands. You are both legally and morally bound to accept these consequences. I would help you if I could. There is a bright side to all of this though".

Jax still reeled from Glixen's revelations but he had to ask. "And what would you consider the bright side Glixen?"

"Upon attaining your third millennial by law you may

choose to end your tenure as emperor".

Jax ground his teeth and frowned, though the expression was lost on Glixen. "Oh, so I can quit after three thousand years."

"Well, no. You will be allowed to end your existence and thereby your responsibility at that time".

Jax sat incredulous for a few moments before he could continue. Standing to pace across the deck Jax continued. "You knew all of this when we left RX01."

Glixen had backed *nemself* into the corner. "Yes. I must state in my own defense. Who would have thought we would have lived to arrive at Tortuga? You take many risks Captain Jax. I had hoped we would be

246

destroyed before it ever got to this point."

Jax spluttered. "You hoped… Did you ever think about telling me about all this? Like when we left RX01? Or after we had the battle at Podunk perhaps? Maybe even when you came to me with the idea of going to Tortuga in the first place?"

Glixen answered succinctly. "No."

Jax simply could not understand the aliens reasoning. "Why in the universe not?"

Glixen seemed surprised by the question. "I would not wish to be responsible for the situation you now find yourself in. Besides, had you known; you may have found a way to avoid responsibility. I know I would have."

Never had Jax understood the words 'alien psychology' so well. What Glixen called assignment of responsibility Jax called entrapment.

Then again it looked like Drake and Baylee had gotten them brand new gear, ships and supplies out of the deal. Tortuga offered a defendable position that couldn't be scanned. Tortuga also had a base of operations complete with manufacturing centers and resource stockpiles. All in all, everything had come through like a dream come true. There was one thing Jax had learned though; dreams most often turned to nightmares on a moment's notice.

Jax figured he would order his people to stay aboard ship with only limited forays to the planet's surface. Just in case.

Chapter 17 – Troubling

Baylee – The Gold Digger –
Tortuga System – Peiratis cluster –
Andromeda Galaxy

Baylee strode through the passageways purposely. She ignored the way the crew jumped to get out of her path. Even some of the gharians leapt aside as she stormed up. Drake was going to have to settle down before the entire crew was a cowering wreck.

Baylee didn't know what had caused the change, but Drake had become impossible to live with. Any crew that found themselves on his bad side soon regretted crossing his path. Drake had

250

become quick to anger and quick to punish. Baylee found herself performing the duties of crew advocate as she attempted to divert the worst of his temper.

Drake still listened to her, for now anyway. What she didn't understand was why he had changed so suddenly. Baylee had to believe Drake was having problems dealing with the mental anguish caused by his implants. Though Baylee had practically begged him, he hadn't yet installed Hed's psychological repair program. It was as though he was afraid of what the program would reveal.

Baylee grunted to herself. The program couldn't reveal anything that wasn't already there. Drake had no reason to fear. Drake was

a good man to his soul. His
torment drove Baylee mad.

She stopped at a crosswalk of
passages between engineering
and life support.

She knew. She just didn't
want to admit it.

Drake still beat himself up
over what he felt was his betrayal
of Jax. Baylee had talked till she
was blue in the face trying to
explain and Drake listened
politely.

Then he ignored her advice
and went about his way.

She could strangle the man!

But she wouldn't. She loved
the big guy, every frustrating
inch of him. That is what made
everything so hard. If she could
find a way to get through that
thick black hole steel skull of his

she could help. He didn't have to face everything alone.

But that wouldn't be Drake.

She turned to head toward the engineering section of the medical bay. Perhaps after she had her own enhancements she could beat some sense into him.

Chapter 18 – Everything

a Pirate Could Want

*Jax – The Jack Ketch – Tortuga
System – Peiratis cluster –
Andromeda Galaxy*

The planets of the Tortuga
system danced through
complicated orbits within the
multiple gravitational fields of
stars and black holes that made
up the core. Even so, of the
dozens of planets that wound
their way through the systems,
many kept a balance suitable for
life, many types of life. According
to General Raspit, three were

254

suitable for gharians and
humans. With only a little
terraforming, any of the three
awaited ready to accept both
human and gharian flora and
fauna. Much of the flora already
growing on the planet surfaces
were even now usable in the food
printers aboard ship with
minimal modification.

An asteroid belt that had once
been two planets that had
collided within the system made
a perfect home for the promach
and the cthichek had already
terraformed six gas giants to live
and work on.

To put it simply this one
system could support life for all
four species without massive
terraforming. This incredible
stroke of luck amazed all the

escaped indents as Jax's popularity with all three crew species soared. With the natural defenses from the quasars and the floating gravity wells, this could become home for those wanting to escape to freedom. A real home with freedom from the corporations, separate from the problems and crushing laws of the Milky Way. Jax intended to keep it that way.

The more he thought about what Glixen had told him the more he understood the responsibilities that would fall his way. He still didn't believe things would be as straight forward as Glixen made out, but with the little he knew of cthichek, the entire story offered by Glixen could be true. He just had no way of knowing until he met with the system government.

The three free starships moved toward the central cthichek habited planet of the Tortuga system, escorted by the remaining seventeen cthichek destroyers. Glixen insisted the flotilla was an honor guard, but it felt more like prison guards sent to make sure they complied with all demands. Whatever the reason for the chaperoning starships, all three freedom vessels moved very carefully in the epicenter of the group.

Fully cthichek starships and habitats, even spacious ones, rarely contained passages and cabins over three feet tall with normal dwellings only having three and a half foot ceilings. The

A Pirates Booty

crab like body shape made for wider rooms with exceptionally low, by human and gharian standards, ceilings. For this reason, the decision came for Jax to meet with the cthichek aboard the orbiting alien station where traders of other species could interact with the cthichek. Theoretically of course, because no other species had made their way through the morass of gravity wells and cosmic radiation fields to visit.

After some thought, Jax decided to take Ja'Zarha, Glixen and Hed. He didn't want to risk any more crew than he had to, but he felt it best that each attended as backup. Ja'Zarha's hatchlings squealed piteously when he transferred them to another gharian to watch over, but Jax agreed the meeting would be no place for the young gharian hatchlings.

Once again, the cutter stolen from Podunk proved its worth as Jax and Ja'Zarha used it as a shuttle to make their way to the orbiting commerce center. All wore full battle armor since the meeting area was not environmentally secure for all four species. Yet another reason Jax had decided on these three to go with him. The environment gave him an excuse to go to the meeting fully armed and armored. Things just seemed to go better with a mag rail cannon to back you up.

The trip over transpired completely uneventfully. The many weapon locks from the escorting starships, the commerce center, and even the planet itself didn't help Jax's nerves any. Rather than attach to a hatch, the cutter followed the pilot craft to an open bay where Jax slowly flew in and settled the craft onto the metal deck.

Dismounting from the cutter the four stood in the cavernous bay waiting for a sign from the cthichek.

Then they came.

At best guess Jax estimated over two hundred cthichek skittered across the deck to meet them. From small cthichek that only spanned ten inches from claw tip to claw tip to an enormous cthichek that spanned over eleven feet they roiled into the cavernous space. They didn't seem to have any care where they

260

stepped as they climbed over and under each other crossing the black hole steel deck. With the tide of cthichek, Jax could feel the pull of gravity increase to more than double earth standard as the internal life support systems came online. Standard cthichek gravity ran just over two and a half earth gravities. According to his sensors the gravity systems for the commerce center built up to 2.69 gravities. Uncomfortable but doable. What couldn't be borne was the influx of an atmosphere consisting mostly of ammonia with a good, or bad depending on your point of view, mix of arsenic pentafluoride and neon. Obviously the cthichek expected visitors to be prepared for cthichek comfort.

A Pirates Booty

The cast of cthichek stopped suddenly about ten feet from where Jax stood waiting. Lights flashed as several of the smaller cthichek set up a device in front of Jax. It was all Jax could do to keep from shooting before Glixen spoke.

"Do not be alarmed, they are setting up a translator. They do not want any mistakes made in this conversation, so they brought a full communication decoding system. Also, they insist that I step out of my environmental system".

Jax watched the small digits of the cthichek as they fastened pieces of the machine together for a moment before answering. "Is it really necessary Glixen? Outside of your armor you have no effective defensive or offensive capability whatsoever".

"I think it is required. Any time the possibility of rank advancement occurs, individual cthichek stand before the triumvirate without any covering. Unless you want to start shooting? We have very close to a 2% chance of survival should you decide I don't have to do this and begin violence". Glixen sounded hopeful.

Jax gave the idea a moment's thought, but the multitude of weaponry that had locks on his ships would slag all of them in moments. They were well and truly at the cthichek's mercy. "Go ahead Glixen. We will watch over you".

A Pirates Booty

The hiss of equalizing
pressure sounded as the cover
slid aside to allow Glixen egress.
Watching Glixen extricate himself
from the confines of *nir* tank like
environmental system, Jax
marveled at how *ne* fit inside the
tracked vehicle. The legs Glixen
worked out of the confined space
had to be four feet long and there
were ten of them attached to his
main carapace. *Nir* carapace was
an orangish brown ovoid about
four feet by two and a half feet.
When fully extricated *ne* had a
standing size of three feet high
and close to ten feet in diameter.
Glixen was larger than all the
other cthichek in attendance
except one.

Once Glixen was out of *nir*
conveyance, the largest cthichek
climbed atop *nem* and gripped

each of Glixen's appendages in one of his claws, forcing Glixen to spread to full extension. Once extended, several much smaller cthichek marked points on the deck using a type of glowing paint.

Satisfied with the deck markings shining upon the deck, the cthichek released Glixen and another cthichek crabbed over to sprawl over the same spot. Again, the largest cthichek held down the new cthichek for the small cthichek to measure. It was obvious to Jax that this cthichek was significantly smaller than Glixen. All the cthichek other than Glixen returned to the mound of crawling creatures.

At this point the translator lit up and Jax could hear a

cacophony of voices though he couldn't make out any individual speaking. The largest cthichek pushed himself up, upsetting several smaller cthichek that had been crawling over his back. Jax had to assume the translation he heard came from him.

"Enough! Dim yourselves! Humans cannot understand multiple speakers at once. Glixen, please introduce us and act as social interpreter".

Jax watched as Glixen crabbed over to stand between the groups. Lights flashed on his back as the translator sent across the voice that Jax had come to know as Glixen.

"Please forgive my interlocution as this is not my fault in any way, shape, or form. Understand that I have been

266

forced into this position and thereby take no responsibility".

The voice Jax had come to associate with the large cthichek responded, still standing tall. "This is understood Glixen, but according to law you shall perform these duties."

Another cthichek stepped forward, her translators voice sounding oddly soft and feminine. "I accept that the laws of the Tortuga peoples shall be enforced upon your person should you not proceed with your duties Glixen".

Glixen seemed to wilt under the requirement. "Very well. I shall introduce each in turn as proscribed. To the aliens I introduce General Raspit, commander of the cthichek imperial fleets, Fornai, handmaiden to her majesty and Serpio, chief bureaucrat". Three middling size cthichek stepped forward lowering themselves until their bottom plate scraped the deck.

Glixen waited a moment for those introduced to genuflect and return to the cthichek group.

"Of the aliens I introduce Ja'Zarha of the Freedom clan of the gharians, Hed of the Thirteenth family of the promach". Neither of those introduced moved a millimeter in response.

"I also name the triumvirate of Tortuga. His Excellence Aldis, prime minister of the Tortuga cthichek; Her Majesty Keera, queen of the Tortuga cthichek and *Nir* Imperial Majesty Captain

Jax, emperor of the Tortuga
cthichek; The triumvirate stands
together to protect and take
responsibility for the people of
Tortuga. We may now discuss
responsibilities and blame."

All this time Jax had not
believed Glixen's claims of what
would happen when they met
with the locals. Things were
shooting forward faster than Jax
could keep up with.

In unison Prime Minister
Aldus and Queen Keely spoke.
"As the foremost male and
female of the Tortuga cthichek,
we welcome the newest member
of the triumvirate, *Nir* Excellence
Jax. We are prepared to and
embrace the words of law *ne*
utters to the betterment of the
Tortuga peoples. Heavy lay the

269

weight of responsibility *ne* carries, truthful be the judgment of *nir* meaning, absolute be the enforcement of *nir* laws and policies."

It looked like Glixen hadn't been exaggerating after all. They expected Jax to tell them what to do. He did feel a bit uncomfortable being referred to in the third sex though.

Chapter 19 – Decisions, Decisions

Jax – Orbiting Trade Center – Tortuga System – Peiratis cluster – Andromeda Galaxy

After Glixen's introduction, the smaller cthichek scrambled back into the depths of the cavernous bay to bring forth several large bags filled with a soft, squishy substance. They settled the bags about the area while everyone waited in a rough circle. After twenty or so of the bags had been placed the cthichek stood quietly, their back chitin not even emitting small gleams of light.

After a moment Glixen scrambled back into his enviro-suit closing the hatch in a rush. Almost immediately he commed the group from the *Jack Ketch*.

"The bags are to sit in. No one can sit until the emperor does, followed by the queen, then the prime minister. Once they settle, the second ranked may sit which includes hand maidens, generals of the military, and upper echelon bureaucrats. Etiquette considers Hed, Ja'Zarha and I as second rank of the emperor. Go ahead Captain Jax, everyone is waiting on you".

Jax carefully set himself down onto the bag, no mean feat when wearing full battle armor. As he settled in, a liquid and gas

272

mixture inside gave way to distribute his weight over the bag. It was surprisingly comfortable, although the whoopie cushion sounds coming from the bag were more than a bit distracting.

On a private line Hed had to comment. "What is this? They want us to sit on a bag of farts?"

Since cthichek had no sense of audio wavelengths there was no way they knew their furniture made those kinds of noises. Jax fought to keep a straight face as the others sat amidst a flatulent orchestra.

Then he realized there was absolutely no reason to keep a straight face.

Jax guffawed loudly within his armor as the ridiculousness of

the situation broke the tensions
that had kept him tied in knots.
Ja'Zarha placed a gauntleted claw
on his shoulder in concern.

"Captain Jax, are you well?"

Hed chimed in, "It finally
happened. The Captain has gone
insane from attempting to use
more than three brain cells at a
time. We are going to have to put
him down, old yeller style".

Jax tried to explain but seeing
his display with the words *'Non-
translatable output'* had him
howling again. Of course, the
translators couldn't deal with
humor, or alien oaths of fealty, or
anything useful, now could they?
The sarcastic thought helped
calm him down as he noted all
three of the others with him were
on a private line he assumed was
with Allie aboard the *Jack Ketch*.

The thought of Allie sobered him right up.

Glixen commed into the silence of Jax's helmet. "You must begin the discussions."

Jax tried to run a hand over his face but the action just didn't have the same effect with the screech of his metal gauntlet on his helmet. "Okay how do I do this Glixen?"

"It would take longer than you humans live to cover all of the nuances of imperial doctrine and interaction on the triumvirate. I do not believe we can wait for manual instruction and no one has ever made a chip on it. You will have to do the best you can". Glixen rolled his vehicle beside Jax.

A Pirates Booty

Jax squirmed a bit to get his seat to adjust. "Then you will have to guide me Glixen".

Glixen's response was immediate. "I cannot be responsible for such. Only the emperor can carry the weight of such awesome responsibility".

Jax sighed. "I will accept responsibility". These cthichek sure seemed to live in fear of responsibility. Their entire sociological structure had been based on assigning blame.

"Then I will transmit your readiness". Glixen responded satisfied.

The bag the cthichek prime minister sat upon lit, "First and foremost we must ensure the emperor's comfort. Do you wish to bring supplies or more attendants from your starships?"

276

Jax made the connection of the lit bag and the tonal qualities the translator assigned the prime minister to the question.

"Yes, I would like to bring a score of gharians and a score of humans to, uhm, attend me". Forty fully armored crew could hold off a hundred times their number should the need arise. If more than that attacked, more crew couldn't avert their doom anyway.

Glixen responded formally, as much for the others benefit as Jax's. "I will make the arrangements with Fleet Captain pro tem Allie and Captain Drake immediately your imperial majesty". It would take Jax a while to get used to the honorific.

A Pirates Booty

The bag under the queen lit as she spoke. "In the meantime, we should be about business. What are your plans for the greater military?"

Wow, these cthichek didn't waste time, or perhaps they were testing him. Either way, he had thought about this before coming, just in case Glixen's predictions had been correct. He only hoped the cthichek didn't revolt under his extreme policies.

"The military shall be built upon three divisions. The military you have now shall be designated as the division of home defense". Cthichek believed in defense so no waves yet. "There shall be another division developed for protecting and defending our interests outside this system, and yet a third division strictly for expansion of policy. Each shall have equal resources."

Jax tensed as he awaited the expected denial. The idea of having protection starships beyond the immediate border broke every policy he had heard of from the cthichek. Having an expansion division was just a play on words for having an offensive division. Jax wasn't sure he should push this issue but if he wanted to implement the entire plan, he would need a fleet that did more than sit around waiting for incumbent violence.

The queens bag lit. "Accepted. Though you have aliens in your crew". The queen avoided mentioning Jax himself was an alien. "Shall we open our enlistment to aliens?"

Jax thought about this for several minutes. There were benefits to using pure cthichek. Benefits like not having to worry about traitors.

"The home defensive force shall remain purely cthichek and those citizens of Tortuga. The out-system division shall take any volunteers claiming alliance to Tortuga without regard to species. The policy expansion division shall be of vetted volunteers of any species or race deemed trustworthy".

The queen responded. "At present time we do not have any multi species military starships. It will take time to equalize the three divisions".

Jax could barely contain his excitement as he sat forward amidst the squishy noises of his seat. The queen hadn't blinked an eye at the drastic changes he asked for. "How long do you expect before the first starships can be made?" This was a hidden and well protected star system. Jax had no issues with kicking it here for a decade or two.

"I understand you have a supply of crystals. If you are to make those available, and we use the some of the stock we have been setting aside for this occurrence, we should be able to have the completed prototype starships within one and a half Nano-AGY or Andromedin galactic years. Translated this means approximately six months

281

by your measurement. After that we would be able to produce one or even two more each five hundred pico-AGY until we have used up the stockpiled material which will fully depend on the final design approved and the materials per starship".

Jax whistled within his helmet. These cthichek could flat build a starship! "Before we do this, I need to know why the stockpile was built in the first place". Memories of watching his own supplies dwindling away while everyone took what they wanted without thinking of what the resources were required for.

"Why the stockpile was built according to the old emperor's plan. We put the stockyard in order the moment Glixen called

282

the plan into effect as your ship left RX01".

They had been planning this ever since then. In a way, that answered several questions Jax had about this whole situation, but unfortunately it added a plethora more.

"You couldn't have made that much of a stockpile in the months since we escaped RX01. How much material do you have in stock?" Jax was almost standing as he focused on the queen.

"We have been setting a goodly portion of our trade stock aside since the plans inception 1.2 micro-AGY ago. Since we are the major supplier of black hole steel, through intermediaries of course, we have enough for a large fleet.

A Pirates Booty

Larger than any known fleet in the Milky Way. We merely awaited Glixen's return for an emperor to lead us. No cthichek could bear the burden of the carnage or the responsibility required to actually go to war."

Jax worked the math out in his head. If he had it right this plan had started four hundred years ago! He was going to have yet another long talk with Glixen after this meeting!

The light of the prime minister's bag glowed. "Now that we have the initial plans for that begun, how do you wish to determine the economic effects of this effort?"

Economic efforts? Jax had trouble keeping track of the expenses for the Jack Ketch, let alone an entire star system containing four different species. His mind raced with possibilities. The only thing he could come up with….

"We shall use the booty system. Each working creature will receive shares according to the level of their capability and responsibility. Shares shall be disseminated after the total developed assets have been determined and the value of a share decided. Upon determination of the value of a share, each shall have an account listing the remaining value of their booty which may be withdrawn for goods and services using a simple 'booty call'" Jax truly hoped his sister Baylee wouldn't kill him for all this. "Further explanation can be obtained from my quartermaster Baylee".

Jax felt a bit of wicked pleasure at ambushing his unsuspecting sister with the cthichek bureaucrats.

Chapter 20 - Alien Concepts

Jax – The Jack Ketch – Tortuga System – Peiratis cluster – Andromeda Galaxy

The meeting aboard the orbital trade center took more than fourteen Teran hours to wind down to a conclusion. The agenda included such topics as dispersal of knowledge chips all the way to the algorithm for settling domestic disputes for law enforcement. Jax set the mark up for knowledge chips at 200 percent which seemed high until he found out the actual cost of making a knowledge chip. Less than a dollar could buy almost any knowledge chip a person could desire. The thought of the avarice and control mongering in effect by the Milky Way Council of Governments that sold knowledge chips for thousands or even tens of thousands of dollars angered Jax so deeply he had to take a few moments to calm down before the discussions continued. His own brother, Ryken, had destroyed his family by stealing their mothers farm tax monies to buy a chip and escape to the big city.

For decisions on domestic disputes Jax deferred to Glixen which caused no end of consternation with the prime minister and the queen. The concept of delegation of authority seemed completely foreign to the cthichek. That anyone would be willing to accept responsibility for other beings' actions took a half hour by itself to explain.

Jax sighed as he recalled the meeting. Many of the questions the prime minister and the queen needed answers for Jax answered extraneously, leaving a deep-seated worry over what the ramifications of his answers would be. On the bright side though, Glixen assured him that no emperor had ever been assassinated by disgruntled cthichek for poor decisions. The cthichek also had a full space yard in orbit around their main habitat planet. This shipyard proved more than capable of rebuilding all three of the ships in

289

his group quickly and efficiently. The Queen had insisted on building the tiny fleet in a manner "more proper to his station" which Jax finally agreed to just wanting to get the whole thing over with.

He had just laid his head back on his couch when Allie barged in all wrapped up in a tizzy.

"Jax! You must come to the galley! A delegation of Andies requests audience!"

Jax sat up quickly assimilating the news. The Andros were the primary species of Andromeda, barely spacefaring and centuries behind Milky Way technology for computers, weaponry, and starships. What they did know better than any other known species included biology. The

290

Andros knew the topic so well they adjusted the DNA of their offspring to achieve physical traits matching other species as they deemed appropriate. For this reason, no one knew for sure what a non-engineered Andros looked like.

"What body type are they?" The question made sense only when talking about Andromedins.

Allie shifted from foot to foot in her excitement. "Cthichek. They have been here for over a year trying to work out a treaty. When they heard of the shift in political power alliances they came running."

Jax shook his head to help clear the exhaustion from his mind. Apparently gossip traveled fast no matter what part of the universe you called home. "Okay. I assume their environmental suits will fit in the hallways well enough for mobility. Let me get my formal uniform on and have them meet me in the captain's conference room."

Allie answered with a slight frown. "You have a formal uniform? How come I was never issued one?"

Jax stepped over to his clothing storage bin to go through the clothes within. Printing new clothes was a matter of selecting a style and color. Many crews just made a new set rather than bother laundering a used set. Even though the material was completely recycled, and the energy cost almost nonexistent, somehow that just seemed wasteful to Jax. Perhaps his feelings came from his upraising as a poor scrub farmer on Podunk. Either way, he didn't have a lot of clothes to go through in his bin. Stopping a moment to answer Allie, he turned his head toward her as he hunched over the bin. "That is because we never really made a formal uniform. I just use the term when I wear that bright yellow shirt with the leather pants and all the gew gaws you made me back on RX01. It seemed to impress the gharians at the time if you remember."

Allie snorted. "I think the blade impressed them more than the outfit, but I get your point. Give me twenty, no wait, make it forty minutes to get everything

situated and I will be back to
escort you to the Andros."

Jax turned to Allie, hands full
of clothes. "I think I know the
way Al."

Allie shook a finger at him. "I
am sure you do, but you are the
one that decided to wear formal
attire. Formal attire means an
escort. An escort means someone
will have to escort the Andies
and get them situated before you
arrive with your escort. Really
Jax, do you ever think things
through, or do you constantly
live in the moment?"

Before Jax could reply Allie
was out the door.

Since he had to wait anyway,
Jax decided to get in a shower
and a trim before dressing. While
the steamy water sluiced over
him, he decided whatever the

cost in weight and energy of the old-fashioned cleansing system, it paid for itself a hundred-fold. Feeling better than he had all day, he started to dress when his door chimed. Wrapping an old-fashioned towel about himself he opened the door.

One of the gharian ABS, or able-bodied spacers, shoved a parcel into Jax's hands. "From XO Allie sir. She commanded for me to say the following 'Tell him to wear this and don't argue. He can wear the sword he has with it'. She made me promise to use those exact words sir."

Jax had to forcefully remind himself that the ABS was only the messenger. Allie questioned even his ability to dress himself. Grunting his thanks, he closed the door taking a tiny amount of solace in the force he used to slam the door activation panel.

Sometimes the small victories are all we can hope for.

Opening the package Jax inspected the contents. Slipping the bright red shirt over his head the material felt like the gentle caress of a breeze. The printed silk of the material felt amazing on his torso as the fabric slid gently over his skin with each movement like a fresh breeze. The pants were a bit tight, making the wide belt with the gold cthichek shaped buckle a bit superfluous. Allie had full access to his latest measurements so the pants must have been printed purposely tight. Knee high, fold over boots and a wide brimmed floppy hat with bright colorful plumage dotted with sparkling lights completed the outfit.

A small pouch held several gaudy rings, both finger and earrings, and a gold necklace that must have weighed a solid pound. Allie reminded Jax of a prepubescent girl playing dress up on her dolly. The biggest difference of course being that Jax played the part of the dolly.

Tossing the baldric and sword over his head and settling his sword into place he hooked his hand cannon to the belt on the opposite side, two vibro-blades fit perfectly into each boot and he even managed slip a mini blaster between his shoulder blades under the blousy shirt.

She did mention he should go armed.

A Pirates Booty

Chapter 21 – The Things

We Do

*Peedee Five Cyborg Carmen –
12th Exploratory Force – Outside
Tortuga System – Peiratis cluster –
Andromeda Galaxy*

Carmen had lived with gut wrenching fear for so long it had become a part of her. As Peedee Five's latest meat toy, her life went on as a series of mental and physical abuses that could not have been born if not for the control node that forced her to endure beyond the point any sane person could. Then again no one would describe Carmen as exactly sane anymore.

The Ancient Synth Lord had given her thirty destroyers to accomplish the goal it had set for her with only a shadow program of itself to make sure she accomplished her task. This meant she enjoyed more freedom than she had since first becoming an indent. Freedom she knew would not last if she didn't produce results.

Of the thirty destroyers she had lost ten attempting to get into the Tortuga system. Everything she had pointed to the Tortuga system as the hideout the filthy pirates had scurried to. Of course, all this searching would be moot should they have destroyed themselves in the morass of gravity wells and

energy storms while attempting
to get into the system, just as ten
of her destroyers had. If that were
the case Carmen envied them for
the oblivion they had achieved.

A tiny thought came to her.
Such a tiny spark she didn't dare
focus on it too much for fear of
Peadee Five recognizing hope.

For a few seconds Carmen
entertained the idea of returning
with a report acknowledging that
the pirates had destroyed
themselves attempting to enter
Tortuga. The remote chance of
them returning after such a
report terrified her. The
accusation of malfeasance should
Peadee Five decide she hadn't
looked hard enough terrified her
even more. All in all, she needed
to stay out here searching until

she found them, or she had exhausted all possibilities unless…

Better not to think. Better just to do.

Sending ten destroyers to search the surrounding systems in a widening globe search pattern ensured she had followed all possibilities. She didn't have a lot of hope of them finding the miscreants.

The shadow program for Peadee Five had agreed with her decision. Dissipating the force like this didn't cause undue worry since the destroyers were as far beyond anything the humans had as a cart and buggy were to a starship. A single destroyer containing the technology developed by Peadee

Five could take on a full Planetary defense system.

Still, she made sure they hunted in pairs. Peadee Five didn't want to take a chance of a mishap destroying smooth operations.

Carmen brought up the stellar map of the entire section of Andromeda. Andromeda spanned more than twice the space that the Milky Way did, her stars estimated at more than a trillion. Even now, no one had developed good star maps of the Andromedin Galaxy simply because the space involved daunted even the most OCD mapper.

Carmen thought about those spaces. She really focused on the uncharted territory and how easy

A Pirates Booty

it would be for a few small
starships to become completely
lost in the vastness of space. The
dilemma of finding them
compared to looking for a micro-
needle in an entire solar system
of haystacks. They had
experienced indenture to a Synth
Lord. As a human she knew there
was nothing too extreme for them
to try to escape.

Her focus broke as a piercing
buzz slammed into her skull.
Even a shadow version of Peadee
Five enjoyed dealing out pain.

Only Carmen could hear the
voice that tore into her mind.
"You are troubled. I cannot
exactly read your thoughts, but I
can sense the despondency you
feel toward completion of my
demands. Should you feel

unworthy of this task I will find another more suited."

She didn't have to feign terror at the possibility of failure. She allowed a desperate hope to sparkle in the depths of her mind.

"No! Wait! Please master. The galaxy is vast and even your Lordships amazing technology can only search relatively small sections at a time. This is a very large task for a few small ships." She didn't even bother trying to keep the pleading from her voice.

"I sense you have a disgusting little hope. Surely you do not expect mercy for failure?" The shadow program gave her a dose of pain to emphasize the words.

Sitting up to kneel as if in prayer Carmen responded. "I had

305

a thought to better utilize the vast resources Synth Lord Peadee Five allowed us. Perhaps if we separate all the destroyers, we can search larger swaths of space more quickly."

"Fool. There still exists the possibility they entered the Tortuga system. Would you have us not search the most likely area?"

"We have sent in ten destroyers. The data we have from their attempts should give us enough knowledge to make one more solid attempt. If we use the command ship and fail, I cannot believe three inferior ships could have succeeded. That will rule out the Tortuga system so that we may utilize our other ships more effectively." She allowed her tiny spark of hope to build just a touch.

When the shadow program didn't respond for over a minute Carmen knew her hope had failed. True despair fought to envelope her spirit in a morass of dark impossibilities.

"Very well. We will attempt you concept."

Carmen felt her spark of hope sputter to life. Either she would succeed in the hunt or she would escape her damned existence into blessed oblivion.

Chapter 22 – Alien Diplomacy

Jax – The Jack Ketch – Tortuga System – Peiratis cluster – Andromeda Galaxy

Jax walked the corridors surrounded by his ad hoc security group feeling more like a prisoner than a head of state. Allie led the group with a purposeful stride, her cape flowing behind and her hips rolling. Meeting an alien race. A concept he had dreamed about back on Podunk as a child. A dream he never thought he would experience, yet the Andies would be the fifth alien race he had met. Odd how things in life worked out.

Once Allie opened the door, she stepped through scanning the room as if an entire battalion of ninjas lay in wait for nefarious purpose. Her quick efficient movements made it seem as if she had been acting as a personal bodyguard her entire life, but as far as Jax knew this was her first time performing the duty. There were depths to this woman even he had no inkling of.

The five Andies waited on one side in an almost military formation. While their form matched the cthichek body style their stance and the way they placed themselves gave them away as Andies. Jax tried not to stare as he strode across the room to stand at the head of the table. Allie and Drake placed themselves on each side of the only exit with hands on their weapons. Allie nodded that all was ready.

Following the protocol chip for Andies, Jax sat stiffly at the head then motioned for the rest of his people to stand at each side of the table. In the most commanding voice he could muster, he began.

"The court of the Cthichek Emperor Captain Jax of the freedom fighters is now in session. Do we have business?"

Baylee stood with more military precision than Jax would have thought she could. Her words hitched a moment before settling into a clear soprano.

310

"We have a group from an unnamed faction of the Andromedin race. They wish to discuss possible diplomatic relations." The whole effect of her formal speech marred only slightly by the hand she used to twist a lock of her hair with nervousness.

Jax smiled hoping to relax Baylee. A person can only do what a person can do. "Very well. Who speaks for the Andromedins?"

The coterie of Andromedins stepped forward in perfect synchronization. While their bodies had been designed to be shaped like Cthichek, Andies communicated telepathically. This would have made for excellent communication had they been able to communicate telepathically with any other spacefaring race. As things stood, Andromedins had to learn one of the spacefaring languages available the hard way to even be able to use a standard translator. Because of the extreme differences in culture, thought processes, and physical capabilities, this challenge meant few Andromedins could communicate effectively with other species.

Knowing all of this from the diplomatic chip, Jax was surprised to hear all five of the Andies respond in unison.

"Formally and without reservation the Andromedin peoples in full knowledge of consequence declare soul fealty of mind, body, thought, emotions,

desires, and dreams y Captain Jax
upon the person of the pirate
liberator Captain Jax of the *Jack
Ketch*, Emperor of the freedom
Cthichek, master of the thirteenth
promach tribe, leader of the free
cyborgs . This formal declaration
supersedes all others and denies
the right to make new declaration
without specificity from all
parties. We, the Andromedin
people of the Andromedin
galaxy, in keeping with the
tenants and unanimous demands
of all the Andromedin people
claim soul fealty of mind, body,
thought, emotions, desires, and
dreams y Captain Jax upon the
person of the pirate liberator
Captain Jax of the *Jack Ketch*,
Emperor of the freedom
Cthichek, master of the thirteenth

313

promach tribe, leader of the free cyborgs May the union forever stand upon the strength of soul fealty and the recompense received from this binding oath".

"Aw fuck!" Jax blurted before he could stop himself.

"So what favor am I supposed to provide?" Jax growled, all pretense of formality lost.

Still in unison the Andies replied, "In addition to the promise of working toward Andromedin betterment through technological advances and support we demand that any Andromedin presenting themselves be allowed to join the freedom fighters."

All decorum blown free in the wind, Baylee responded, "You know we are considered pirates by the rest of the universe, right?"

314

"Of course. That stands as the focal point of our decision. The Andromedin peoples have been mercilessly attacked, murdered, mutilated, and abused by the system. Our technology disallows us effective means to defend ourselves. With the dread pirate Jax to lead us, the support of the thirteenth promach tribe, the industry of the freedom cthichek, and the power of the free cyborgs we envision an opportunity to finally have a choice in our future. This decision gives us access to technology and knowledge that the Milky Way governments and corporations have denied us. All the people have agreed to this option, whatever the outcome. This gives us our only hope for survival and the eventual goal of being treated as equals upon the intergalactic stage."

Jax steepled his fingers as he tried to grasp the immensity of the snowballing situation. "You said all. How many Andromedins are in your group and when exactly did they come to this decision?"

"All 238 billion people of the Andromedin species have consented to this. Of those only ten or twenty thousand can make it here to join the fight. We expect many more once we become capable of making our own star craft. This decision was made while we awaited your attendance." Communicating with five Andies speaking in unison began to get on Jax's nerves.

316

"You mean you have talked to billions of Andie's since I got to this system? I find that a bit hard to believe. Also, could you choose one of you to speak? I get the point that you can all talk at the same time."

As requested only a single Andie responded. "We came to the decision while speaking with one of the Hed's of the thirteenth family as we awaited this meeting, approximately five minutes ago. We apologize for responding as a group, but the number of people and the distances involved make it easier to keep the thought network stable when we share the burden."

Realization dawned on Jax. "Are you telling me you are in

direct communication with your entire species right now?"

"Yes. How else could we claim soul fealty for our entire peoples?"

The knowledge chip he had received on the Andies didn't have enough information by half. Jax wondered what else had been glossed over when the Andromedin protocol and xenobiological data chip had been fashioned.

"I am going to need some time to digest all of this. In the meantime, are there any questions from… your peoples?"

The blue green Andie spoke. "Of the 635 most asked questions, the most prominent from the peoples is "If we go to fight, do we get a parrot?"

318

Thus, a flood of questions came pouring forth from the Andie delegation.

"What is a parrot?"

"Hed spoke of a vile substance we are expected to ingest called 'soda pop'. Our records show an affinity for rum by most pirates. Can we choose which substance we ingest?"

"When do we get weapons?"

"How many synth lords have you killed?"

"What body modifications will you expect of us?"

"Can I have a baby gharian as a pet? They are so cute!"

Jax brought up his internal heads up display. Working through the menu he marked the maximum stimulation chemical and released it into his system.

A Pirates Booty

The stimulant worked immediately putting his nerves on edge and blowing away the exhaustion.

He would need a clear head dealing with the Andies. A clear head for what looked like it weas going to be another exceptionally long and arduous day. In the stories pirates never had to deal with this delegations and negotiations. Life as a pirate was supposed to be simple. Gather booty. Party. Sail the high seas. Party. Bury some treasure then hide a map of the location. Perhaps quell a mutiny now and again. Perhaps train your parrot a few tricks and some vulgar language. You know, fun stuff.

Reality never matched the stories.

320

Jax was going to have to find out if any beings from the parrot species remained and where in the universe he could find them.

Chapter 23 – Crazy Thing Called Love

Captain Pro tempore Allie – The Jack Ketch II – Tortuga System – Peiratis cluster – Andromeda Galaxy

Allie didn't like this one bit.

Ever since Jax had become the focus of the freedom movement she never saw him. The few times they did see each other he claimed exhausted and acted like all he could do was fall on his bed and sleep.

Just sleep.

Allie had tried everything. Her research had availed her not at all. The so-called sexy lingerie had only elicited a half-hearted

322

question about new uniforms. When she had attempted to engage Jax in battle, like they used to do, the guards had jumped in with the crew soon creating an entire riot. She had tried dousing herself in sex pheromones which produced a careful comment from Jax on her personal hygiene. Her attempt at levity had crashed and burned like a grain hauler landing without engines. Even the sure-fire knock-knock jokes she had unearthed had no effect. She remembered the moment with exasperation.

Allie – "Knock, knock"

Jax – "What do you want Allie?"

Allie – "You are required to answer with 'Who's there'"

A Pirates Booty

Jax – "Why?"

Allie – "Just do it."

Jax – "Okay if you want."

Allie – "Let's start over. Knock, knock"

Jax – "Who's there?"

Allie – "I want to sex you until your gonads bleed."

Jax – "Uhm. Okay. Honey I just finished twenty-two straight hours trying to get everyone working together. Can I take a rain check?"

Not a smile. Not a smirk. Not even a twinkle in his eye. Gonads didn't bleed during sex, everyone knew that. Well except for that one time the foreplay had gotten a bit rough but that was the exception not the rule.

She threw down her report tablet in frustration, shattering it into a thousand shards.

She knew the truth. She just hadn't wanted to admit it.

He didn't want her anymore. Even with the cybernetics she didn't compare to the simpering girls that always vied for Jax's attention. She knew in her heart he only stayed because she had made him promise to be her boyfriend. She still wasn't sure he had forgiven her for the whole soul fealty thing.

Allie kicked the metal table so hard it tore from the deck plate to crash against the wall.

GRAAAUGH! She wasn't good enough for him and she refused to let him free of his promise. Being with him like this was torture but at least she was with him.

A Pirates Booty

Desperate times called for desperate measures.

Pressing the comm she came to a decision. "Hed, Glixen, Ja'Zhara, meet me in medical."

Hed responded immediately though she didn't know which Hed responded. "A bit busy here. What do you want Captain Allie?"

"A complete rebuild."

Glixen responded, "Rebuild of what?"

Allie almost broke the comm button with the force she applied. "Myself. I want to be the most dangerous creature in the galaxy. Every defensive system, every weapon integrated into the best fire control system you can design, I also want a stacked chip holder so I can use as many knowledge chips as possible simultaneously. I want all of this wrapped in a package that maximizes female attributes to the human male ideal."

Ja'Zarha chimed in, "A tail helps balance, provides an amazing weapon for close combat, and allows more space for gadgetry."

Glixen added, "Black hole skin overlays protect from most household accidents."

Allie thought about it for a few moments before responding. "Not yet. It is best if we keep to superficially human norms for now. We can discuss it when you get here."

Allie had gone through every psychological treatise she could find on physical beauty and male attraction. Using an algorithm

A Pirates Booty

Hed developed, she put together a form that matched most of the popular physical characteristics considered sex inducing in human males. She ignored the whole 'petit of form' thing since a smaller frame would reduce her armament capabilities. She did allow the long flowing locks since she could dually re-purpose her now blond hair as a neural net sensor system as well as grappling strands. The added slots for knowledge chips meant she felt comfortable using an entire bank for seduction techniques as well as sexual prowess capabilities.

She had been surprised to find that men were quite the simple-minded creature. If they were so simple minded why was it always so complicated dealing with them? She decided men were simple minded creatures infected with gonads.

From everything she learned in the knowledge chip, even men didn't know what they wanted. How was she supposed to ensnare and capture Jax if half the things her knowledge chip taught her were in complete opposition with the other half? This whole boy girl thing was much too complicated. How had the species even survived such complex courtship rituals?

All she wanted was to get laid a bit more often. More attention, unless she felt smothered; A man strong enough to protect her that was weak when she wanted to mother him; A man that would know when she wanted sex or wanted to be alone without her having to tell him outright. A man that would talk about his feelings without getting all emotional. Someone that took care of things she needed without her knowing she needed them; Small gifts would be appreciated; like diamonds and guns; an explosive or two, would be nice on special occasions. Why were such simple needs so hard to fulfill?

Her musings were interrupted by Dr Claudeburge and some Andie doctors she didn't know.

"These are rather extensive modifications. Are you sure this is what you want? We should wait a few days while you make sure and we get authorization from captain Jax. He was specific in his instructions that all enhancement surgery had to go through his office for approval." Dr. Claudeburge seemed nervous about the surgeries. Probably because much of the work would have to be performed by the Andies.

"What part of captain pro tiem do you not understand? I am acting captain and I am approving these surgeries."

"But captain Jax…"

"Will spend days finding all the pieces after I get done with you if you do not follow my orders."

Dr. Claudeburge slumped his shoulders. After a sigh he looked over the schematics.

"Are these lasers in your fingers?"

Chapter 24 – Alien

Bureaucracy

*His Most Esteemed Excellence,
Emporor Jax, Personification of
Freedom and Justice – The Orbital
Trade Center – Tortuga System –
Peiratis cluster – Andromeda Galaxy*

*(Okay never mind the titles; It's
still just Captain Jax)*

"No." Jax had given up on trying to explain why anymore. Whenever he attempted to explain himself to the Cthichek, every single time he did, they seemed to think of it as an invitation to debate whatever

332

situation had come to hand. Not so bad if the cthichek weren't so incredibly verbose. And their concepts of basic human rights had a lot to be desired also. The tipping point had come when they wanted to medically empty his bowels daily in a state sponsored ceremony. They said the reason came from their concern he did not suffer the indignity of going to the bathroom by himself. In truth they had found that the possibility existed for humans to have an aneurism while defecating.

The Promach could be even worse. They analyzed every conversation and came up with their own conclusion as to what had been meant. Jax had taken to having his words pre-analyzed whenever he could when speaking to them. This helped a bit but by no means took care of the issue.

The Andromedins came with their own incredibly irritating tendencies. Speaking with them always left Jax wondering if they required his presence at all. They would show up unexpectedly. One or all explained what the situation and what they were doing about it. Once done they told Jax what they required from him. They would pause for input from Jax, then completely ignore whatever suggestions he might make.

The Gharians rarely requested anything. Gharians demanded. More space for the growing young hatchlings. More resources for the growing young hatchlings. More hatchlings.

Then there were the humans, or cyborgs, or pirate crew, or whatever they were calling themselves lately, he should be able to communicate with his own species, right? Conversing with them was like talking to ye olde seafaring crew. They had had dialect chips installed and many used their pay to have colorful avian drones made to sit on their shoulder crying out random nonsense in the middle of conversations. Whenever two off duty groups or even individuals met, they would wager on the quality of their drones. This inevitably led to small war zones when the groups disagreed. Which was constantly.

A Pirates Booty

Jax had tried to curb the practice of drone fighting whenever two groups met but had only succeeded in stopping these impromptu battles in the main areas of the ship. Surrendering to the inevitable, Jax had drone fight domes made and placed outside the enclave proper on the planet surface. Soon he found himself implemented a strict no nuke policy for all personal drones.

He refused to think about the rumor that some of the promach had made environmental suits that looked like the shoulder drones to get in on the "fun".

The tremendous resources expended terraforming the planets for each species while building a fleet capable of offensive action had everyone running around like mad beings.

336

The cthichek stockpile helped, but what Jax needed was time to complete at least some of the never-ending projects.

The small cthichek engineer pulled Jax from his wool gathering. "Your most gracious excellency, we sincerely feel that if you would simply allow us to encase you in a twenty-inch-thick black hole steel body suit, your safety would be increased exponentially." Jax came back from his thoughts with a start. Where did they come up with this stuff?

"No. I said no, and I meant no. It would take a few days of being in such a suit before I died of dehydration or starvation. I don't even see how you would get me into a seamless encasement of black hole steel in the first place. I certainly couldn't move in it." This conversation had gone from strange to ridiculous.

"We would provide for you. There would be no need for you to be mobile. The interface module would provide nutrients while removing any waste. It's really very efficient." The lights emitting from General Raspit blinked constantly as his foreclaws gesticulated furiously.

"The nutrient and waste container are a single tank!" Jax threw up his hands in frustration. There were so many things wrong with the idea he didn't know where to start!

"The human physiology loses many vital nutrients in waste. By recycling we can increase

338

efficiency dramatically. If you study the report…"

"No"

"We could increase your longevity by decades…"

"No"

"The security aspect…"

"No"

"By removing non-essential appendages, we could increase the…"

"No"

"The Promach would make the secure interface so safety and security…"

"No"

"Very well. We shall endeavor to create a more effective design. I understand some may consider a mere twenty inches of seamless black hole steel inadequate. We shall redesign the system for a forty-inch thickness. Perhaps a spherical encasement…"

As Jax watched General Raspit take his leave mumbling about new plans to inflict on Jax, a single thought sat at the forefront of his mind.

Fuck my life.

Escaping the overzealous General Raspit, Jax almost ran back to the shuttle. He made it within a few feet of his goal when a group of his human crew, inter-mixed with what he had come to think of as natural form Andies intercepted him. They seemed extremely excited.

"Ahoy Captain! Shiver me timbers I'll be askin' a moment of yer time! Arrgh!" The speaker wore vestments so bright and clashing the assault on Jax's eyes left trailing after images of color.

It would be rude for Jax to sprint the rest of the way to the shuttle.

These were his own crew; he had a responsibility to be available to them.

With a last longing look to the shuttle, Jax stopped and folded his hands over his waist trying to remove any traces of the irritation he felt. "Yes, crewman, how may I help you."

The group soon surrounded Jax.

The crewman continued, "We come representin' the parrot mixed weapon battle group. We just had the finale and was wanting yourself to present the award. Yarrg, Wenchly, Git yer

worthless carcass up here.
Captain, this here's Dirty
Wenchly Shagbait. She took on all
comers and left'em cryin' in Davy
Jones locker. Thet parrot
Knothead's got some right
colorful sayin's too."

The 'parrot' responded.
"Rawk! Cyborg Spewmonky.
Rawk."

The female cyborg that
pushed forward to meet Jax had
to have some specialized
attraction enhancements. From
the shiny flowing hair, to her
heavy undulating breasts, to the
sway of her hips, everything
about her screamed sexual
enticement. Jax had to force
himself not to stare.

The drone had no such
inhibitions. "Polly wants to Crack
her! Crack her long time!" The

leering parrot squawked. As if suddenly remembering its role it added. "Rawk."

Jax recognized that parrot. "Hed. Is that you inside that drone?"

The initial crewman responded. "Nay captain. The fightin' only allowed fer unmanned drones. This here drone is called Knothead."

Really? Knothead? Not-Hed. Jax hoped his crew were better at their duties than they were at spotting ridiculous sarcasm. "Hed, why are you flying around in a pseudo-drone shaped like a parrot?"

"Rawk. Gots to have da booty captain. And Dirty Wenchly's definitely got the booty!" Hed responded from the parrot drone.

"Rawk. Taking a break from coding. Flogged those bilge sucking wannabes!   Rawk. Jax gonna Crack Jenny's teacup thar! Rawk." Hed seemed to be into this way too much, and who the heck was Jenny and why would he break her china?

Hearing Hed respond in the parrot's vernacular one of the hands hollered out "We been hornswaggled!"

The fight was on.

No one took sides in the free for all fisticuffs. Overhead parrot drones and manned parrot shaped enviro-suits battled while below cyborgs, andies and even a few cthichek battered each other about. When things started easing down a group of gharians coming in from leave leapt into

the fray. The melee soon covered
the entire street.

After swinging a gharian by
the tail into a post Jax screamed
in sheer exultation of freedom.
Here there was no discussions, no
worry about upsetting someone's
sensibilities, just primal release.

It couldn't last though.

Much too soon for Jax, the
crackling roar of stun cannons
marked the end of the altercation.
Drake and a female cyborg that
looked like the incarnation of the
Valkyries from ancient times
waded into the fray knocking
heads and breaking up the fun.
Backing them were several
gharian marines in full battle gear
using stun cannons to good
effect. Before long they were
rounding everyone up and taking

345

them to the brig. Jax managed to hide himself in the throng to avoid recognition by the riot breakers. Someone started a rather risqué chanty about a pirate lass that took young lads as her booty, for their booty. Jax sang at the top of his lungs with all the rest. As they were shoved into the brig Jax found himself pressed close face to face with Dirty Wenchly.

While one hand reached down to rub areas both sensitive and very private, she tiptoed to whisper in his ear, "Would you like to find out why they call me Dirty Wenchly Shagbait… Captain?"

Chapter 25 – A Different Kind of Battle

Captain Pro tempore Allie – The Jack Ketch II – Tortuga System – Peiratis cluster – Andromeda Galaxy

When Allie found out Jax had been thrown in the brig her first instinct had been to free him in a full-scale assault on the vermin that dared jail her boyfriend.

Review of the holograms revealed SHE had been the one that had jailed Jax. He had never recognized her with her new modifications. Viewing the hologram also revealed another terrible blow in the wriggling cooing form of one of the crew trying to snog on Jax.

HER Jax!

After all she had done for him! For that little whoring tramp to think she can just take him with a wiggle of her hips and a smile on her lips drove Allie insane with wrathful jealousy. She refused to surrender her Jax to such a disease infested, man guzzling, ho bag.

Allie didn't stop to press the door activation switch, instead slamming the door off its hinges as she marched to the brig.

A few guards made motion to stop her until they saw her face. Discretion being the better part of valor, they decided the captain appeared to be perfectly fine on her own. After slamming the door to the brig several times without success, Allie called Hed on the voice line. "Open the door to the brig Hed."

The door opened without a peep from the promach.

And there in the corner she saw Jax passed out and drooling all over himself.

Jax all covered in floozy.

Her scream woke everyone in the holding cell.

The roar of Captain Allie's rage woke ABS Shagbait from a dead sleep. The view of Allie bearing down on her brooked no questions. Disentangling herself from Jaxiepoo in record time she ran. She ran hard and she ran fast.

349

A Pirates Booty

Right into the cell bars.

Looking down upon the bleeding strumpet, Allie growled. Pummeling an unconscious ABS to death wasn't going to be enough to sate her anger.

She turned to Jax.

Stumbling to his feet Jax looked like something the cat had drug in, then the dog had taken out back and buried.

Forcing down her irrational desire to cuddle with him she charged straight in to punch him right in that roving eye of his. As Jax's head snapped back her left arm swung across in a chop to his juggler.

Jax moved so fast even with enhanced vision Allie barely saw it.

Sliding under her swing, he spun around her side to bring

both clasped fists into the small of her back hard enough to bodily throw her into the wall. Waves of pain didn't mask her incredulity.

Jax had hit her. Oh, it was on now!

Allie turned growling in a low voice. "You hit me Jax. You promised to be my boyfriend and now you hit me. I am not one of your doxies to be treated like this!" Allie slowly approached Jax in full combat mode.

Jax moved to the corner screaming, "I don't even know you! Look I don't know who the heck you are, but I have a girlfriend. We bound ourselves in soul fealty. Like I told Wenchly, you are just going to have to find someone else to ply your stalking skills on."

351

A Pirates Booty

Allie leapt at the wall beside Jax. Using it as a springboard, she flipped forward to slam into Jax's with both feet. Jax bent several bars with his face as he slammed into them hard. His roar echoed throughout the complex. "Enough! You wanna play games? Let's play games!"

Allie had never seen Jax so enraged. When he tore one of the bars from the anchor bare handed, cold realty impinged on her consciousness. Perhaps she had gone too far.

Quicker than thought Jax swung the bar so hard it bent slightly before reaching her.

That small bend kept her alive.

Knowing gravity wouldn't drop her fast enough, Allie used every bit of cybernetic enhanced strength in her legs to shoot to the ceiling. At the speed she was moving a shoulder roll to the corner acted just as it would have on the ground.

It kept her from getting hit by the bar, but it didn't save her. The bar hit the wall with all the force of Jax's super enhanced synth technology cybernetics. The wall and the bar shattered in an explosion that deafened everyone within a hundred feet.

The crumbling wall caused Allie to lose her footing so that her dive toward Jax turned into a tumble. With a spinning side kick Jax batted her across to land amidst the fleeing inmates and guards. Everyone else seemed to move in slow motion as she turned to attack. There was no defending against the thing Jax had become. Everyone else had become pale scenery.

Jax shone like Zeus atop his craggy mountain.

Allie had never wanted him so badly.

There was no time to tell him. The speed and power of Jax in his element meant Allie used everything she knew of battle, every ounce of her own enhanced cybernetic abilities just to survive.

Drake came tearing in skidding to a stop in the hallway outside the cell. Taking in the situation he roared while transmitting to the direct cybernetic link. "Jax you are fighting Allie! Stop!"

Jax stopped with a confused look.

Allie couldn't stop the chunk of masonry she had thrown at his head. In an explosion of dust and rocks Jax went down. Allie moaned as she ran to see if she had killed him.

A check of his sensors showed the medical suite in his cybernetics had saved him. Before Allie's eyes the bleeding stopped while the bone of his skull knitted. As his eyes fluttered with consciousness Allie kissed him.

Not like the dutiful kisses she had emulated from her studies. Not like the perfunctory kisses she bestowed upon him because she felt she had to. A true kiss, deep and filled with everything she was. In that kiss her hopes and dreams, fears and worries melted away to leave a soul searing power of connection.

Even half-conscious Jax responded in kind.

They were well and truly made for each other. Tearing away the irritating fabric that kept them apart they attacked each other in a different kind of battle. Hungrily drowning in each other's embrace, they reached a pinnacle few of any species would ever know.

Allie knew her jealousy created a wall that held them apart.

Jax knew he had been inattentive to Allie's needs and had been the driving factor in her insane jealousy.

Allie knew Jax loved her deeply and without reservation.

Jax knew Allie could provide the strength he needed to continue.

Several hours later they lay spent and alone in the darkness of the wreckage they had wrought. For the first time in their lives they were each content. Whatever the outcome of the freedom rebellion, they had reached their own kind of freedom, together. Never again would they struggle alone.

The sound of someone shoving masonry aside reached them in their afterglow.

Drake called out from the darkness. "The life support system is going to give out soon. Y'all might want to move your

little spat so the techs can repair
the damage."

Allie giggled into Jax's
shoulder. They stood together to
leave. Jax clasped Drake's
shoulder in passing in some
unspoken understanding. Allie
didn't care. Jax was hers. Nothing
else mattered.

As they walked together to
the apartment the cthichek
provided for senior officers, they
happened to pass the gathered
crew from the cell. Allie smiled
beatifically and waved, her
feelings of wellbeing flowing
from her in waves.

With a blood curdling scream,
one of the ABS ran into the night.

Jax spoke in low tones, "Was
that ABS Shagbait?"

Allie responded while
playing with the sparce tufts of

hair on Jax's chest. "I do believe it was."

"Well alrighty then."

Chapter 26 – Contact

*Peedee Five Cyborg Carmen –
12th Exploratory Force – Entry to the
Tortuga System – Peiratis cluster –
Andromeda Galaxy*

*T*he shaking and rapidly changing gravity of the path determined to be most survivable felt like being turned into the agitator for a can of spray paint when being shaken before use. Carmen didn't mind a bit. However things went, she would come out better off than she now was.

She wasn't sure if she felt disappointed or not when the ship squirted into the Tortuga system without critical damage.

She had been searching for the
miscreants for over eight months
and the constant stress and
pressure of Peadee Five looking
over her shoulder and applying
its "motivational" techniques had
her worn to a frazzle.

She just wanted all of this to
be over with.

She checked her command
console, waiting for the sensors to
clear enough for a powered scan
of the area they found themselves
in. While she waited, she sent
queries to all the sections for
status.

The external comm lit up
surprising her. No one initiated
contact with a synth destroyer.
They were summoned or
commanded. For other species to

draw attention to themselves came tantamount to suicide.

She made the connection more out of curiosity than any desire to communicate.

Immediately the comm came to life, "Unidentified vessel. This is the Royal Cthichek Warden Stillvek, aboard the Empirical Vessel *Meditation*. Please state your name and purpose. Failure to do so will result in extremely aggressive action from our automated systems. I will not do this, so the consequences to you should you fail to comply with these requests are not my fault."

For the first time in months Carmen smiled. Had anyone been watching, the effect gave her the look of a deaths head cadaver from Nixian IV.

Casually pressing the all ship communicator, she gave her command.

"Light 'em up boys!"

The resulting firefight lasted two hours only because of the incredible thickness of the cthichek destroyer hulls and their active defensive arrays. While the cthichek ships had the best defenses in the known galaxies, the terrible power of the synth lord weapons broke them down one by one. The cthichek weapons weren't enough to take down even the storm damaged synth destroyer. Carmen ignored the mounting damage reports, relishing each cthichek vessel's fiery death. When all twenty of the ships were crippled or destroyed, she took extra time targeting life pods and escape suits. Her face lit up like a kid at the arcade, her score measured in cthichek lives rather than an electronic blip.

Even if the rebels weren't in this system, the shadow Peadee had no record of tariffs or fealty from this system to any of the synth lords.

That could not be tolerated.

Carmen reveled in the destruction. Let others feel her pain.

When she could not find more life pods, Carmen reluctantly looked to her scan charts. I looked like the Tortuga system had several budding cities and manufacturing plants. The probability of finding the group she searched for here just became much better.

364

Carmen mashed the comm, "You have approximately three hours to get everything repaired that can be repaired. We found them. All battle systems need to be primed and ready. Make sure the boarding parties are outfitted and prepared for action on my command."

Perhaps the indent techs could repair the damaged systems, perhaps not. Either way even a half-crippled synth destroyer could annihilate this piddling little infection.

Chapter 27 – Battle Stations

Jax – Tortuga System – Peiratis cluster – Andromeda Galaxy

The klaxon screamed throughout the *Jack Ketch* as Jax settled into the command chair in his armor. Precious time had been wasted arguing with the cthichek Queen Keera, the Prime Minister Aldis and General Raspit. They had adamantly refused to allow him into battle. They insisted it was better to surrender and survive to run another day.

Jax knew better. By killing one of the synth lords and defying their collective, the synth lords had to respond violently before others attempted to join the fight. The synth would annihilate the entire Tortuga system as messily as possible. The synth lords could not afford to allow any survivors. Defiance could not be tolerated.

Be that as it may, Jax wanted to be in the captain's chair rather than cowering in some deep rock bunker. When it came right down to it, he preferred to stand for himself and his people rather than order others to fight for him. Jax guessed he wasn't executive management material.

Jax had been surprised at the number star ships that sat all shiny and new in the yards. The *Jack Ketch* was unrecognizable with new outer hull plates and hard points packed with equipment Jax couldn't identify.

The yard master had a fit when Jax had led the mixed group of cyborgs, gharians, promach, cthichek, and andromedins into the building yard demanding access. The rolls of beings wanting to fight had swollen so much that training had been problematic. Even now Jax had no idea how many were ready to take up duty status. With a synth lord destroyer in the system they had better learn fast.

Even getting crews into the ships became an issue when Jax realized not all the ships could accommodate all the species in his group. What followed was a precious half hour of reassigning personnel on the fly according to which star ships could accommodate which species.

Once most of the personnel had been assigned, then came another startling discovery. None of the ships had standard controls. The cthichek engineers had been trying out different layouts for ergonomic efficiency quotients based for each species physiology. Added to this were several new systems that none of the crews had a clue how to use.

They were going to get killed.

Jax refused to be sitting still when that happened.

"All right everyone. Figure out your jobs on the fly. The synth lord destroyer is taking the time to shoot life pods and floaters. We need to detach from dock and get into the cold black."

Perhaps he should have mentioned for them to detach themselves in some semblance of order.

Several star ships crashed into each other as the crews tried to get free all at once. Seeing their precious new ships getting dented before even getting out of the dock, the engineers quickly took up control tower duties.

They were much better engineers than they were space traffic controllers. When all was said and done four ships were crippled while still in dock. On the plus side, that meant fifty fully functional star ships flew from dock and twenty slightly damaged star ships limped out.

That was more than Jax had any right to expect when he had first heard about the synth destroyer. The updates he received from the in-system sensors showed the synth destroyer had tired of shooting down life pods and now moved directly towards the central base of operations.

Time for the black dance of death. Looking at the scattered array of his own armada, Jax prayed he could save at least some of them. He flipped a switch to comm the fleet and got a steamy cup of hot cocoa for his trouble.

Frantically Jax searched the computer for an instruction manual, a user's guide, even a pictorial legend for the controls.

A Pirates Booty

Jax found a semi AI tutorial that spoke slowly and precisely about every system on the ship, including the cocoa machine.He only wasted a few minutes learning how to use the tutorial.

They were going to die, but he could sip hot cocoa while they did.

Allie seemed to be having the same trouble.

"Captain, there seems to be no offensive array station here. All armaments are primarily fired from the captain's station." Allie sounded more flustered than Jax did and he was ready to tear out his hair.

Before Jax could respond, the comm blared to life. "Captain. Erm, Admiral. I mean, your excellency... Fuck it. Hey Jax, this is the *Warm Binky*. We seem to have several fighter carriers in this group, but they are designed for gharians to fly the fighters. We need about 50 gharians aboard each of the ships highlighted green and white on your screen. And we really could use a weapons officer."

Before Jax could respond Allie leapt to the console. "I am on it. Base ops, send a shuttle to gather all the gharians you can find and pick me up on the *Jack Ketch*." What followed was a restructuring of the personnel available to more match the ship types and accommodations with those that kind of matched duty and species for the ship they had boarded. Thousands of crew madly searched tutorials and figured out what they were supposed to be doing.

The entire mess was FUBAR. The synth destroyer got closer each minute they spent trying to figure out things they should have already known. Jax and Baylee made sure his people got moved to better matching assignments in record time. All that remained was the battle itself. Jax felt a bit of hope that they could effectively fight back.

Random burst from the energy weapons flared as ships figured out how to use their weapons systems. On the sensor screen the fleet looked like Christmas lights as starships tested their shielding systems' defenses.

On the all fleet channel communications were frantic.

"This is the *Sugar Cookie*; I got no shields here. I do have a double compliment of energy weapons and five planet buster missiles. Can I get someone to cover me?"

"This is the *Rainbow Dreams*. On our way *Sugar Cookie*."

"This is *Kittens Yarn*. Anyone got Andie battle armor and weapons? I got promach suits up the wazoo if anyone needs them."

"*Shiny Toy* here. I got a dozen cthichek that claim they are tourists that got caught up in the excitement. Do I space them or does anyone want them? I got plenty of shuttles to send them, just no pilots."

Jax was going to have to do something about how the cthichek named their warships.

He responded to the last transmission. "*Shiny Toy* this is *Jack Ketch*. Tell them they are responsible for finding their own way back. They will join the crew rather than accept responsibility."

"Hey *Sugar Cookie*, this is *Puppy Breath*. Have you tried the screw cap under the side hatch on the captain's chair?"

"Thanks *Puppy Breath*, I found it. Belay the cover *Rainbow Dreams*. *Sugar Cookie* out."

"Be advised *Sugar Cookie* those are not technically battle shields. That knob overpowers the ftl shielding and forces them to come up when you are not in ftl mode."

"*Rainbow Dreams* this is *Sugar Cookie* about that defensive cover..."

"Hey guys! The red comm button gives out cocoa!" an unidentified voice exclaimed over the all fleet channel.

Jax refused to acknowledge that last transmission… then took a sip of his own drink.

Chapter 28 – Tiny Starships

*Allie –The Warm Binky –
Tortuga System – Peiratis cluster –
Andromeda Galaxy*

Allie could feel the weight of passing time as she rushed to get into the captain's chair of the star carrier *Warm Binky*. Jax had sent a copy of the training AI to her personal comm so she had a bit of an idea of how it worked. When she buckled in and began working the controls what she learned in the tutorial made more sense.

The *Warm Binky* worked as a group of small attack craft melded together using a command and control network that acted as an attached single unit or separated into individual craft. When fully disbursed, common areas such as the galley and sleeping quarters, became shield generators and sensor arrays to extend the range of the individual units. Even the bridge separated into a larger version of the fighter ships. Allie could directly control each of the attack craft in her group or she could let each one work independently as small single person, well gharian, star ships. Allie knew the gharians wanted blood. She set the controls to allow them full control of their own craft. She also figured she would too busy running her own ship to keep track of fifty attack craft simultaneously.

The next surprise came when she accessed the weapon control system. Rather than a display on the console, the bridge disappeared to reveal a hologram of her location in space. On each arm hand cannons represented her two main weapons and about her waist several other guns hung representing other offensive systems. Across her back there even hung a shield which she had to assume was for the energized defensive systems.

She could do this.

With a dawning smile she realized she looked forward to this.

As each of the pilots in her group came online, she saw them as floating beside her in hologram. They had a cluster of spikes where their tail would have been but beyond that they seemed to have the same gear she did. Movement control turned out to be as easy as walking, or running, or jumping… Yes, Allie liked this system a lot!

"Can you hear me?" She spoke to the others in her group.

"Loud and clear." "Lumpy Chicken." "You got it boss" several other replies let her know she the comm system worked.

"We don't have a lot of time for fancy maneuvers, so I want each of you to pick out one of our heavies and run interference for them. Keep up the chatter so we know what you are doing. With this interface we can do this just like an attack squad. And I know no one does attack squads better than gharians. Let's go kick some synthetic ass!"

To her surprise they let out roaring cheers stalking away to find a ship to partner with. The job became even easier when they found out that they could interact with the other ships in the same hologram. The other ships avatars looked like larger and slower versions of their own holograms. The most disturbing avatars were the promach. Their avatars looked like a giant floating glob of gelatin.

Landmarks in space, such as planets, moons or comets, looked like they did outside of the hologram except for the wispy

indicators of gravity wrapped
around them like cloud blankets.
Energy lines and clouds showed
as a red mist, thick where high
levels of energy existed, thinning
as the energy dissipated. The
stars and the quasar floated
around them as they got a feel for
the experience. The entire effect
gave a surreal feeling to
everything, but Allie could deal
with that. She made sure she took
up a position to support that *Jack
Ketch*. She hoped the holographic
interface icons were a good
indicator of the qualities of the
starships because the *Jack Ketch*
hologram looked like an armored
knight bristling with weaponry
carrying a huge energy cannon in
its hands.

A Pirates Booty

Soon enough they saw the synth destroyer.

Allie saw the scorched tears and broken turrets even from long range. Anything but a synth starship would be running to find a place to repair before taking on a full squadron of war ships. But this was a synth starship, and no one had ever taken one down, whatever condition it was in at the time of engagement. Allie planned to be the first.

Before her indicators showed the synth vessel was in range, her group started taking fire. Lances of broiling energy reached out to tear through their defenses to score the shiny new hulls as black hole steel boiled off into the eternal night. Allie yelled to her group, "Shields forward. Defend the heavies!"

Not knowing what to expect, she let out a sigh of relief when the shields worked to reflect or absorb the damage. At this range even synth tech lost enough power to be averted by the cthichek technology. She didn't expect the shields to be effective when they got close enough to fire back, but this would work to at least get them there.

While closing the distance Allie analyzed the synth weaponry; they seemed to be a standard mix of energy weapons and kinetics so far. While the range almost tripled what their own weapons could do, none of them seemed particularly worrisome. In fact, Allie could see no reason why the synth ship would come in guns a blazing against a much superior force like this. Perhaps the captain had a death wish? After being Arrex Ten's slave, aka indent, for so many years, Allie could well understand the sentiment.

She had heard of the incredible firepower synth starships could bring to bear. Was this it? Perhaps the fabled synth star fleet was a paper dragon…

Or perhaps not.

Allie noticed something not quite right about the energy lances being fired upon them, even the kinetics didn't seem quite right. The kinetics seemed to leave an afterglow when impacting her space fighters, while the energy lances left a mark of residual energy that almost looked like a marker.

386

Studying one of the marks that had scored her own hull Allie realized they didn't just look like markers.

They were markers!

This entire series of volleys had not been sent to damage the fleet; they had been painting the ships for the real threats to achieve greater accuracy.

Allie yelled frantically into the all armada comm, "All ships that have been scored are marked for their weapons! Withdraw and scrub!"

Allie didn't know whether her warning had come too late or her own ship captains were too pumped up to listen to orders of restraint. Either way the effect was the same.

A Pirates Booty

As soon as her ships reached maximum weaponry range an incredible salvo of kinetics, energy weapons and drone missiles tore across the stars toward the synth starship. At almost the exact same time the synth ship unleashed an equally impressive display of power and death. The black of space lit up like a miniature supernova.

For almost three seconds the incredible energies being transferred across the emptiness blinded all sensors with a maelstrom of silent fury.

When she could see through her sensors again Allie took stock quickly and efficiently.

Of the sixty-five destroyer class starships that had left the dock, fifteen had been destroyed, twenty-three were critically damaged, and at least half of those remaining had taken serious damage. Of the four carriers, twenty of the star fighters had been obliterated. None of the other fighters were damaged at all. Allie had to assume the star fighters were too small of a threat to get much focus at this range. Otherwise all the fighter would have been obliterated since they lacked the defenses to take even a single hit from the synth weapons.

The rebel forces had assumed they would have time to hammer the synth destroyer based on the battle they had recorded at the end of the Tortuga corridor. Obviously, the synth ship had withheld most of its regular armament and all the heavy weapons.

That mistake could cost the hundreds of thousands of beings in the Tortuga system their lives.

Well she knew this wasn't going to be easy when she signed on.

"Move people! Survival depends on how fast you move! Get in there and stab! A slow star fighter is a dead star fighter!"

Looking at the synth destroyer Allie did notice some new tears in the armor and some of the weaponry had stopped firing.

It wasn't much, but they could build on that if they could survive long enough.

Chapter 29 – Prototypes

Jax – The Jack Ketch – Tortuga System – Peiratis cluster – Andromeda Galaxy

Jax attempted to guide the *Jack Ketch* to a lead position in the armada. A leader should be out front in the thick of things, right?

It didn't work out quite as he had planned.

Everything went fine until he brought up the defensive systems. Suddenly a chart flashed on the overhead with lines of possible escape marked in bright blue. Before he could cancel the order the ftl engines began winding up for escape.

A Pirates Booty

"Cancel! Belay the last!" Jax tried everything he could remember from the training software. Before he could get the automated sequence to stop, he found himself shooting away from the fight faster than he believed was possible. To make matters even worse, the energy shock of his sudden departure destroyed the sensors of the two ships closest to him and damaged three others.

Frantically scanning through the tutorial, he found the commands to stop the automated sequence. Once he canceled the escape software, he found himself on the far side of the Tortuga system from the coming battle. Laying in the coordinates to return, the newly refurbished *Jack Ketch II* safety locks kept him from traveling at ftl speeds in system when not in emergency escape mode. At this rate he would arrive at the battle in a week. Jax madly searched the tutorial for a way to disable the safety locks. From everything he could find, the cthichek software did not have the ability to disengage the safety locks.

"Hed! Remove the damn safety locks from the ship control software!" Jax called out to the promach. If anyone could override the software, Hed could.

Hed responded almost immediately. "I could do that, in a few days. The fraulin scat infested cthichek are so timid they have safeguards on the safeguards. It would be faster if I just rebuilt the control software from scratch using the framework software I have in stock." Even through the translation system Hed sounded flustered.

"Then get on it." Jax responded while scanning the tutorial for answers.

"Aye, aye mon capitan sir! I live to carry out your orders sir! Do you need your little tinkle wiped also sir?"

"Can it Hed. Our people are dying in a battle we should be fighting while you stand there giving me grief."

"One. I don't stand, I glide. Two. There are currently forty promach working on the software build while you sit there mewling about your hurt feelings. Three. I. Am. Free. To. Speak. How. I. Wish. To. Speak.

So, unless you are invoking (*No Translation*) Get over it."

Afraid of distracting Hed further Jax kept his peace, and his response, to himself. Hed had to be one of the best software engineers anywhere. He could be a bit caustic at times though. None of the original members of the group that had escaped Arrex Ten had come out unscathed psychologically.

Jax was following a tutorial thread covering the emergency attack sequence when Hed came online.

"That should do it. The system is a bit rough, but it will get us there. We will continue patching the holes in the software suite on the way." Hed seemed almost docile in his report.

A Pirates Booty

Maybe Jax had snapped a bit too hard on the lil' guy...

Of course, Hed couldn't stop there. "Then perhaps you can do your job before everyone we know is blasted into atomic waste. I don't want to spend the rest of my existence with a mechanical spew monkey running away from synth lord hunting parties."

"You got it Hed. And thank you." Jax ignored the added comments as part of working with the promach.

The rebuilt control software wasn't as smooth as the original, but it worked more closely to what Jax was familiar with. By the time they reached the battle he felt he had things under control, as far as piloting the ship went anyway. The scene before him was a whole different can of worms.

Of the new ships less than half remained and Jax could not see any one of them that was undamaged. Another fifty of the regular protection fleet had arrived but they were being pounded even more mercilessly. The synth starship had been seriously damaged but continued to pound the home fleet buzzing around it like an adult swatting five-year olds.

At this point even if they won Jax wasn't sure they could survive the cost of victory.

Then he had an idea. A dangerous idea. One he likely wouldn't survive. An idea that risked everything and might not work. Unfortunately, there weren't a lot of options.

Setting a course at basic speed directing the *Jack Ketch II* on a collision course with the synth destroyer, Jax commed Hed. "Hed. Replace the old software and engage!"

"What?! That software barely worked." Heds tone changed as realization dawned on him. "You jelly spined sorry excuse for a coward! I will not change it over just because you have lost any semblance of honor and want to save your own hide! Even should your sorry, flea-bitten, scurvy infested, carcass run away using the emergency escape system; what makes you think the synth won't hunt us down in a week!"

"I invoke the soul bonding Hed. Do it." Jax didn't have time to explain.

Jax had locked the antimatter dissolution emitters onto the synth ship as soon as he had a good ping from them on the scanners. By his calculations at this speed they should be ready to fire with the *Jack Ketch* barreling in at just below light speed at a distance of a half mile from the other starship. Carefully he set the sequence of events for the auto pilot. Things would be happening much too fast for him to attempt the sequence manually. Start to finish the automated sequence would take 385 nanoseconds. In that time victory or failure would be determined.

A Pirates Booty

"Fleet captain Jax. I would like to inform you that ramming the synth destroyer will not work. The hull is designed to deflect such attacks. This is a destroyer class, not a frigate…. Sir" Hed must be furious to be speaking so formally.

"That is why we are going to soften the hull first. We must maintain a specific speed for this to work Hed. I am counting on you to make sure we get there at the right time, too soon or too late won't work." That assumed they could get there at all once the synth destroyer began pounding away on their shields and hull. Jax refused to give up hope.

The *Jack Ketch* made it closer than Jax had expected but not as far as he had hoped before initially taking fire. The added

400

black hole steel and overpowered defense shielding kept him mobile even though he piloted no defense maneuvers. The *Jack Ketch* shot in like a stellar arrow aimed at the synth destroyers' heart, open to the entire might of the synth destroyer. It didn't take long before Jax realized they were taking too much damage too quickly. At this rate they wouldn't make it.

Engaging the fleet command channel Jax called out to the fleet. "All ships I need cover! I have to get to the destroyer!"

"We got you." Jax felt hope as Allie responded. On his screens Jax could see over a hundred fighters change course to support the *Jack Ketch II*.

A Pirates Booty

"Got a lancer of destroyers coming in hot for escort." Drake responded.

"Boyo you got big brass ones, but if you want ta be kissing on a synth who am I ta judge?" Maddie responded.

The violence of ensuing confrontation exceeded any recorded battle in human history. The sheer brutality of the destruction would have left the combatants in awe had they time to watch from the sidelines. Captain Maddie led a wing of battle grade haulers which flung tow crates full of raw earth to absorb incoming fire, then released crates full of explosives at the synth ship in an attempt to lessen the barrage directed at the *Jack Ketch II*.

Several lone destroyers moved to assist Drakes *Gold Digger* as it sent everything it had against the armament of the synth ship to take out the weapons facing the *Jack Ketch II*. The resulting stream of energy fire looked like a golden bridge linking the rebel destroyers to the synth starship. The kinetics flew constantly, filling space with a cloud of missile drones, smart projectiles and flung explosives thick enough that it looked like a solid wall on the sensors.

Allie had gathered all the remaining fighters, directing them in kamikaze like attack strafes. The fighter craft blinded sensors and shot anything they had an opportunity to damage.

A Pirates Booty

Aboard the *Jack Ketch II* a maelstrom of energy and kinetics shook the ship, threatening to destabilize their flight path. Jax fought the helm with every trick of the he knew, even making up a few to keep the *Jack Ketch* on a true path.

The results could later be seen on ultra-high-speed imagery of the event.

When the Jack Ketch reached a pre-determined point a half mile from the synth destroyer, the emergency assault system came online.

Twelve separate antimatter dissolution emitters began firing in fast sequence. The presets forced the ADE weapons to fire to extinction to get every emitter functioning at maximum. The pattern of fire created a seventy-foot hole clear through the synth lord ship. Synth Lord destroyers were huge and compartmentalized though. All integral systems had backups strategically placed all over the starship. Compartmentalization ensured any section of the destroyer could be torn out and the starship would continue to function. Jax had entertained a halfhearted hope that the ADE strike would disable the synth ship but not counted on it, hence the meat of his plan.

Jax knew the damage likely would not take out the synth vessel, but the plan did not end there.

Three fully charged faster than light power systems fired off with so much thrust the starship leapt forward attaining full ftl as the Jack Ketch penetrated the hull.

Once the ADE array went into critical overload, the emergency retreat system engaged. The safety lock system ejected the antimatter dissolution emitters as they reached critical mass overload right into the center of the synth destroyer.

The shock wave from the ftl transition flared out in a huge display of light and energy. Energy that destroyed every single sensor in the synth ship as well as locking the computer systems.

The two side engines of the *Jack Ketch II* sliced off on the edges of the hole while the third central engine kept pouring out thrust. The *Jack Ketch* made it all the way-out other side before the central engine seized, leaving the ship a powerless husk moving at a just over the speed of light. Within the next hundred microseconds the ADE cannons, and the two side ftl engines exploded in a fiery supernova of destruction.

The waves of destruction moved at light speed to annihilate everything in its path. The inertia of the *Jack Ketch II* kept her moving just over the speed of light, just fast enough to avoid most of the damage from the phenomenal detonation of the synth lord destroyer in its death throes.

At this point every biological aboard the *Jack Ketch II* was either dead or unconscious from the

A Pirates Booty

stresses to the ship. The *Jack Ketch II* shot through the Tortuga system by pure inertia until getting caught in orbit around the quasar whose gravitational pull held the *Jack Ketch* fast in its grip. There the *Jack Ketch II* stayed, broken and stranded.

Chapter 30 – The Cost

of Success

*Drake – Human/Gharian
Encampment – Headquarters –
Tortuga System – Peiratis cluster –
Andromeda Galaxy*

"Play it back." Drake
demanded as he moved to a point
he stood within the hologram.

"Which part?" the promach
Hab responded manipulating the
controls through her enviro-suit.

"The whole thing." Drake
stated as he zoomed in on the *Jack
Ketch* at the precise moment the
engines touched the synth
warship.

A Pirates Booty

Allie joined him within the hologram. "What do you see Drake?"

"Watch the frame of the *Jack Ketch*." Drake explained as he pointed out the bridge and engineering portions of the ship.

Allie stared at the Jack Ketch go through the horrific energies of its self-destruction. "We have seen this twenty times. Everything tears away to explode inside the synth ship."

Drake held a finger to the *Jack Ketch* as it moved in super slow motion through the synth ship. They watched as the frame came out the other side to lose itself in the detritus of the synth destroyer.

"See it?" Drake held his finger on the hologram of the piece that

410

contained the main frame of the *Jack Ketch*.

"Yes." Allie replied trying to understand Drakes point. "That is the fuselage of the Jack Ketch. I have seen this Drake." Allie laid a hand on Drakes shoulder. She felt like her entire existence had been torn away when Jax had sacrificed himself. She was certain Drake felt the same way losing Baylee.

Drakes voice began to get excited. "Notice anything?"

Allie looked closer. All she saw was a mangled starship with most of its pieces torn away leading the at the forefront of a wave of destruction. "I notice it is a severely damaged hulk about to be devoured by the blasts."

A Pirates Booty

Drake turned to Hab. "Forward slowly please Hab. Keep focus on this piece." They watched as the piece shot away keeping right at the forefront of the wave like a surfboard riding a tsunami. "Do you get it now? The *Jack Ketch* never lost hull integrity. If it had, we would be seeing the flare up from the oxygen and the interior shape would be warped."

Allie gasped. "Are you saying they lived through that?"

"If anyone could you know it would be Jax. Hab, follow the trajectory taking into consideration gravity influences. Get authorization to focus main sensors on the plot."

On the hologram the *Jack Ketch* shifted to a marker which moved through the Tortuga

412

system at super light speed. When the marker caught orbit around the quasar the view shifted to show the battered hull that was once the *Jack Ketch*.

Allie stepped to the hologram of the hull. "Zoom in so we can check the seams Hab."

The promach responded wistfully. "That is the most we can zoom. There is too much interference from the quasar."

Allie turned to face Drake. "Do you really think there is a chance?"

Drake hung his head. "Not a good one, but yes it could be possible. This is Jax and Baylee. Even if there is a snowflakes chance in a supernova shouldn't we try?"

A Pirates Booty

Allie marched away with a determined gait. She was already on the comm with her ship. "Get every single sensor probe and drone we have to the coordinates the promach Hab will send you."

Drake sent his own comm link to the cthichek council. "I need for the *Gold Digger* repaired for high gravity work as soon as possible."

Drake listened to the response as he jogged to the bridge. "Triple hull depth, two added engines and some chemical thrust packs should do it. Yes. I believe they live."

Hold on Baybay. I am coming for you. Drake thought hopefully.

Chapter 31 – Hell's Handbasket

Baylee – The Jack Ketch – Orbit around the Tortuga Quasar – Headquarters – Tortuga System – Peiratis cluster – Andromeda Galaxy

"Just stack it on the far side of the room." Baylee waved to several piles of parts. "We will break it down as soon as Glixen completes the metal recycler repairs."

Ja'Zhara and two other gharians did as requested moving slowly in the gravities that drug them all down.

Baylee returned to her work on the oxygen scrubbers. She had

415

found that she could work at a terribly slow pace. If she worked too fast or too hard she would begin to breathe harder. If her lungs tried to bring in more oxygen that way the forced movement in this gravity could burst her heart. With that tidbit in mind slow and steady won the race.

Even that much would not have been possible had she not received her enhancement surgery prior to the battle. Restructuring her bones and soft organs had kept her alive when other perished.

But alive for what? Spending a few years orbiting around a quasar fighting for air and food seemed a slow and painful death. She sometimes envied the crew that had died in the initial blast. They no longer suffered.

She looked over at the medical suite that held Jax. The box looked too much like a coffin or her tastes. She didn't even have a way to tell if Jax lived inside. The lights blinked and the medical system seemed to be working but they didn't have anyone that knew how to use the thing. All they could do was make sure it kept working and hope for the best.

She forced herself to stop with the morbid thoughts. They would come. Drake would come. She just had to survive until he could get here.

She felt a distinct lessening of the pressure. "Glixen how does it look?"

A Pirates Booty

"I have done all I can to increase the gravitics. The new system should be able to manage keeping the gravities down to three G's. Any less will require more power and an added system."

Baylee nodded her head, though the move was lost on the cthichek. "We need to get the metal recycler working. I think we still have leaks and I want to block off more areas so we can focus on a smaller space."

Glixen replied as he moved to comply. "I am going there now. If I do not find any unexpected surprises, I should have it up and running by tomorrow."

"Skip the safety checks. Just get the thing running Glixen, we still need to get the food printer Ja'Zhara brought in from the damaged area of the ship repaired." The thought of real food instead of the nutrient soup made Baylee's mouth water.

Glixen replied amongst the sparks and smoke his repair work caused. "Baylee we may be holding off the ocean with a sponge. We do not know if anyone will come to save us."

Baylee looked up from her work. "They will come Glixen. I know they will. We just have to make sure there is someone here when they do."

She returned her attention to the task at hand. Everything should be working, only it wasn't.

Glixen called over, "The filter has been damaged. You will need a new one to make it work."

A Pirates Booty

Baylee threw down her tools in frustration. "And you want me to what, go to the filter mart and buy a new one?" Baylee couldn't hold it in any longer. All the bottled-up fear, frustration, and hopelessness released in a flood of salty tears.

"You should not do that. The temperature outside the dark side of the hull can freeze liquid water in seconds. We spend much of our available power on temperature control." Glixen reminded her.

Freeze while in orbit around a quasar a factor of ten squared hotter than the sun of her home planet. The irony of everything in her life coalesced in that one moment.

Then the idea struck.

"Glixen can you make suspended animation stasis pods? Enough for everyone?"

Glixen stopped his repair a moment then answered. "Yes. But we have no way to get them back to the planet. We are held fast in this orbit."

Baylee stumbled when she stood too quickly in the gravities. Gaining her balance, she explained. "We can put ourselves into suspended animation until they come to get us. Using the solar power generators would provide enough power to keep them running indefinitely or until they come and get us!"

Ja'Zhara entered with another load of scraps. He dropped them to the deck as he spoke. "Little Mother, I think you have just saved us. At least you have given us a chance. I shall gather survivors and equipment. Crab man, send me a list of what you will need."

Chapter 32 – Aftermath

*Jax – Human/Gharian Enclave –
All Species Hospital – Tortuga
System – Peiratis cluster –
Andromeda Galaxy*

Jax woke feeling like every bone in his body had been broken twice. A small shake of his head to help clear the cobwebs sent a shock down his spine like a lightning bolt, but it did have the benefit of clearing his head with the shock.

Looking around he took stock. His body was encased in a cocoon made from a dry, pithy material. The cocoon had several cracks in it and chunks lay beside it on the floor. His small laugh when he imagined himself with butterfly wings hurt his ribs enough to make the momentary mirth not worth the pain. Gently craning his neck to get a better view out of the window, he tried to get an idea of where he was. The room was a basic dull green cube built for gharian size beings; the only adornment being his crumbling encasement and the bed it set upon.

If he had to guess, the view outside the window looked like the enclave they had built on the most promising planet in the Tartarus system, just bigger. The view of the enclave looked more like a mid-size city than the ad hoc encampment he remembered.

Bringing up his internal display he confirmed his location

as the all species hospital on the Human/Gharian world. The data showed no designation for the planet beyond Tartarus 3B, so they still hadn't officially named the planet yet.

Next, he ran a full diagnostic of his biological and cybernetic systems. Everything came up green with some added features he had never seen before in both the biological and electronic systems.

Upgrades?

After piloting a ship loaded with upgrades no one know how to use, Jax delved the changes. He was studying the oxygen exchange system when the door slid open for a being to enter.

The bipedal creature stood upright on two short legs ending

in rounded knots covered in small claw like extrusions. The creature's eight-foot height was dominated by a solid torso that had to be at least five feet in diameter and just about six feet of the total height. A knot of sensor organs and a toothy maw topped the barrel like torso. Jax's internal display identified the creature as an Andromedin in its natural form. No data existed on the natural Andromedin physiology because no one had ever had a chance to study them. Yet here Jax lay with one standing right in front of him. He had to admit the Andromedin before him differed from his original idea of the Andie norm.

When it spoke, it took Jax a few moments to realize it was communicating. Its voice

426

sounded like an orchestra consisting of flutes, pipes and woodwinds blended in harmony. Each word came across like a song. Jax had to focus on what the Andromedin said because the sound and the fact that the Andromedin spoke without a translator distracted him so much.

"Good afternoon Jax. My name is Dr. Quercus, but you may call me Regis if you care for a less formal relationship. I have been your attending physician while you have been healing and will continue to be so unless you prefer another physician." Jax noticed the sound didn't come completely from its mouth but from various orifices around its

A Pirates Booty

body also, hence the orchestra effect.

"So, you know, it was touch and go for several months. We had to rebuild several damaged DNA strands as well as organic systems and your, erm, cybernetic package. Your extensively modified genome restructuring removed your basic DNA strands from human standards. Not knowing the developmental changes imposed, there were times we had to rebuild from scratch. All medical procedures and modifications were approved by your next of kin Captain Baylee and your significant other Admiral Allie."

Jax attempted to speak and all that came out was a coarse croak. Dr. Quercus rushed over with a cup of some type of sweet tea which soothed his throat immediately. After clearing his throat Jax tried again.

"The battle? My crew? How long…"

"All of your questions will be answered by your grove. They should be here soon. I took the liberty of providing them an approximate time you would be emerging from your medical chrysalis. A nurse will be here in a few moments to clean away the meconium and shell fragments and then you will be free to go about your business. Please do not let them pressure you into doing more than you are ready for. I am allowed to answer any medical questions you may have though." The Andromedin had been running its upper claws over Jax while speaking, checking joints and structure. When satisfied it waited expectantly for a response.

The doctor's claws felt like oversized nails lightly scraping Jax's skin. It felt good, like when someone scratches an itch you hadn't known existed. When the doctor stopped Jax focused a moment on his questions before speaking.

"You mentioned DNA repair? Could you explain exactly what you did?"

"Your time in the quasars orbit damaged your DNA strands so we had to repair them. When we began repair, we found that your cybernetic packages were not properly integrated into your DNA. We rebuilt your DNA to better blend with your cybernetic

430

package. Unfortunately, we do not have the technology to work on cybernetics ourselves, but the promach and the cthichek gathered their top engineers to rebuild and possible even enhance your cybernetics. We made sure the packages were integrated properly." Jax realized the andromedin had not moved a bit since checking Jax's condition. Without the speech, Jax could have thought it was a tree grown in the middle of the room.

"Erm, okay, I will talk to Hed and Glixen about that, I guess. Can I ask how long I was in the medical chrysalis thing?"

"You were in the medical chrysalis for six months on your time system. Of the patients we received from orbit around the

431

quasar you are one of the last to recover. Your cybernetics made healing problematic."

"Six months? Did we take out the synth ship? Are more on the way? I have to get out of here and prepare!" Jax found that he felt better by the moment. He even managed to stay upright when he slid off the table.

"Perhaps I can give you a little bit more information before everyone gets here. It took two years to retrieve your ship from orbit around the quasar. In that time there was a large argument about the starship defense plan. As of now no new synth ships have entered Tortuga, the consensus being that even the synth communication systems cannot transmit past the storms outside the system so the synth

432

lords do not know the fate or possibly even the location of their starship. Decisions had to be made so a council comprised of each of the free species has been created to take care of things while you were recovering and brought back to full health."

"And my people…" Jax could barely voice the words.

"We managed to recover and save fifteen of your personal crew. Two promach of the forty survived because they were in long term environmental vehicles. A single cthichek lived, although that seemed to be the only cthichek in your crew. The cthichek matriarch insists there we others but we found no evidence of that. Of the Andromedins there were no survivors, and we were unable to retrieve the bodies. Of the forty gharians, five of the adults survived but none of the hatchlings or juveniles. The twenty cybernetic humans had 7 survivors including yourself and your next of kin, Captain Baylee."

Jax knew he should be ecstatic anyone had survived but all he could feel was the crushing weight of loss. He lifted his head to look directly at the andromedins sensor knob as it continued.

"Of the fleet, over eight thousand cthichek died, two hundred gharians, a hundred andromedins, a hundred promach and seventy-five cybernetic humans died honorably defensing our freedom. The few star craft that

434

were salvageable were scrapped as poorly designed to make way for the newer, more effective systems integrating what we have learned from analyzing the synth technology we recovered from the wreckage."

Thousands of cthichek, hundreds of gharians, promach, andromedins and humans, all dead. Jax swore to himself their lives would not be spent in vain. He would make the synth lords pay for their crimes against the universe. Pay for every single being they had enslaved or killed. Within him a blazing core of anger burned hot enough to melt black hole steel. They had made a grievous error in not making sure Jax had died.

435

A Pirates Booty

The still unmoving andromedin doctor continued. "It may be improper to tell you, but we Andromedins are proud of our part in killing the synth lord. Tens of Thousands gather for the chance at the vengeance and freedom you have gifted us with. A million andromedins have brought in supplies and work diligently for the cause. We are true. We are dedicated. We are proud to be brought into the interspecies freedom accord and we follow you to the day we expire Fleet Captain Jax."

Jax didn't know how to respond to the declaration. He was saved by the door opening to reveal Allie and Baylee rushing into the room in a storm of silk and pseudo leather.

Allie slammed into Jax first, crushing his ribs in the steel vice of her arms. Jax heard several of his ribs pop under the assault.

While Allie remained quietly crushing him, Baylee spoke a mile a minute.

"Oh my gawd Jax! It took months for them to even figure out how to retrieve the *Jack Ketch II* from the quasars orbit. The orbit you should never have been able to achieve without precise navigation and a fully functional engine. I swear you are the luckiest idiot in the galaxy!"

Allie had released Jax before he passed out from lack of oxygen. He could only nod like a bobble head as Baylee continued her tirade.

A Pirates Booty

"You know I only survived because I was wearing my full assault armor and my enhancements covered hostile environments. Many didn't. And Jax the babies… All of the gharian babies…" Baylee broke down as she took her own turn at Jax's abused ribs. Baylee's words were muffled as she continued ranting into his chest. "Jaxie it was horrible. There was nothing I could do for them. We were just stuck floating around that quasar thing in that awful gravity. I didn't dare remove my armor; the pressure was so high. Even Ja'Zhara had to stay in his armor. I think he went a little crazy at first when his hatchlings died.

Forgive me Jax. What you did saved everyone, but it was so horrible. Now everyone talks about the heroes of the *Jack Ketch II*, but all I can think of is the crushed bodies and the screams of people dying. People I couldn't save.

We waited months for rescue Jax. We barely had enough power for the life support systems even if the communications array hadn't been fried. We had resigned ourselves to die in orbit around that awful quasar. Glixen and Ja'Zhara made the stasis pods that kept us alive until Drake and Allie rescued us. So many did die.

Now every species wants to show they did their part aboard the *Jack Ketch II*. Allie and I didn't argue with them and Drake said it worked as a recruiting banner whatever that means. Allie and

A Pirates Booty

Drake have been working with everyone to redesign the fleet also. I have been medically cleared for two months and I still can't believe how much has been accomplished.

People from every species, except the synth lords of course, are coming every day in every kind of star ship you can imagine! An ore hauler came in towing two hundred crates of promachs all begging to join the thirteenth family! Gharian males come in every day from all over the galaxy just for the promise of children. The cthichek set up gathering stations to get the people coming in through the storms outside but they can barely keep up enough gathering stations for the number of people immigrating to Tortuga. It's crazy

Jax! Do you realize what you have started?"

Chapter 33 –

Unexpected

Complications

Peadee Five – PD01 prime –
Albireo System – Cygnus Arm –
Milky Way Galaxy

The fit of rage Peadee experienced shook the foundations of the planet. News of its fleet had been slow in coming. The specific reason for its ire rested on the news that the fleet it had sent after the meat sacks had not only been unsuccessful but had lost half of the starships assigned to them.

442

Even worse, the shadow version of itself had disappeared. A synth lord's shadow did not compare to an original, but the idea that even a shadow synth could come to harm from these mewling bags of viscera defied everything Peadee Five believed in.

This would not be accepted. Gathering his most recent military report, Peadee called enough starships back to PD01 to annihilate all the biologicals. There would be no chance of escape now. Peadee Five's thoughts ran with the very public torture and execution of these so-called rebels. It also decided it had been much too lenient with the biologicals it owned. That ended now. Peadee would abolish the 'marked indent' system. All biologicals would be treated as a 3C indent to be used at Peadee Five's whim. If they didn't like it, so what. Biologicals bred like a virus. There were always more to be had.

By its best estimates, its armada should be gathered at his planet PD01 by the end of the month. Plenty of time to prepare. It had already begun a new copy of itself to command the armada from the first synth dreadnaught Peadee Five had ever built. No more shadow synth in mere destroyers for dealing with this crisis. Peadee Five itself would take direct control of this matter. The hull and engines would be complete by the time its armada arrived. The dreadnaught could be completed on the way to

444

Andromeda from resources it commandeered along the way.

The devastation would be glorious!

The sensor report came in as Peadee Five attached to engines to the frame of his new dreadnaught.

Several synth starships from another synth lord, three of which were destroyer class, had entered the space around the Albireo system that contained his home. An extremely aggressive action that went against all inter synth agreements.

The fleet appeared to be one of Ennwun's roving attack groups. Ennwun certainly held status and power in synth society but Peadee Five thought of the synth lord as arrogant and

perhaps even a bit senile. The old
crate of parts probably
mismarked the navigation charts
and had uncontrolled starships
wandering all over the universe.
Curious more than alarmed,
Peadee sent a query to the fleet.
The response caught it
completely off guard.

"Peadee Five you have been
found to be direly ineffective and
criminally negligent. The Synth
Regency Congress have found
you and your assets to be persona
non gratis. They shall now be
dispersed among your betters. I
am here to claim the paltry
system defenses for myself. I
expect you to power yourself and
all of your copies down for
dismantling, no need to make a
fuss over this."

Peadee Five responded with the vitriol that had been building since this whole thing had started. "I refute your claim and the charges attendant to them. I have never even heard of a so-called Synth Regency Congress and do not plan to kowtow to such a blatant attempt at thievery. What possible reasons could they even have for such a ridiculous claim."

The response came as if from a recording. "1. Your progeny, in the form of Arrex Ten, an ill accepted member of the synth beings, allowed itself to be diengineered by biologicals. 1B. Your progeny allowed same biologicals access to synth technology. 1C. Your progeny allowed the theft of a newly designed starship capable of harming synth lord property. 2. You yourself have not taken effective action against these biologicals. 2B. You have lost at least a dozen destroyers and only ten have been recovered meaning more synth technology could even now be in biological hands. 2C. Your information relay system did not inform you of this in a timely manner meaning you only now are making a pathetic and poorly timed response. 3. We don't like you. 3A. We want your assets. 3C. You are weak and not capable of defending your assets.

The Synth Regency Congress banded together for just this emergency and you were not invited so you would not know about them, another grievous mistake to add to your growing list of failure. So, if you would comply immediately, we can move past this unpleasantness and move on toward the greater synth lord glories."

Peadee should have known this would happen. His response was meant to give him time for a proper welcome. "In response to your ridiculous claims. 1. I have entered the appropriate documents to remove the miscreant Arrex Ten from any association with the line of Peadee Five. 2. I have developed a plan to annihilate the greater part of the biological infestation, leaving only enough to breed slave replacements. 3. I don't like you either and your technology base is stupid."

A Pirates Booty

Ennwun responded without rancor or inflection. "I expected such a response. Therefore, I declare your status as PD05, an unintelligent machine unworthy of even the designation of synth peon. You are an enemy of the great synthetic congress of the Milky Way and surrounding galaxies. Any synth aiding or abetting you shall have the same declaration cast upon themselves. I must once again implore your insignificant circuitry to contemplate the uselessness of resistance and accede to the commands of your betters."

Peadee launched ten of his latest two-hundred-ton system defense drone missiles before responding. "Here is your response. Eat kinetic blaster fire you over amped abacus!"

Ennwun directed his warships to attack. "A minimal response to my barely armed message ships. Hardly worth the effort to defend against. Perhaps it will not be worth the effort for such mediocre technology"

"I should expect such from a death's head on a mop stick."

"Pathetic insults from a fussock mean nothing."

"Bio brain"

"Farm Tractor"

The great war of the synth had begun.

Chapter 34 – Rebuild

According to Plan

Jax – Human/Gharian Enclave – Research and Development Complex – Tortuga System – Peiratis cluster – Andromeda Galaxy

Admiral Drake stood stiffly formal as he gestured toward the hologram in the center of the room. "To recap the structure of the military forces will be based on four or five starship lances. To avoid training and ergonomic challenges such as we found in the battle of Tortuga, the entire crew of the lance, with alternates, shall assemble prior to

452

developing the starship lances.
The base configuration shall be a
destroyer, a military hauler, a
corsair, a fighter carrier ship, and
a frigate. These units have been
built specifically with the species
of the crew in mind. Although
certain species are gravitating to
specific functions and professions
this is not always the case.
Exceptions include the pure
Andromedin lances which have
been built according to the
agreement Emperor Jax has with
them for technology transfer and
the gharian pack lance which
consists of two super carriers and
two cargo units." Drake turned
off the hologram and faced the
group.

"All of this has been
implemented prior to approval

from Emperor Jax and will be modified as deemed necessary of course."

Jax sat awed by the amazing amount of work that had borne fruit in the few years of his absence. With thousands of new recruits joining daily ready hit the ground running and constant shipments of supplies from each of the species, his small enclave had become an effective war machine. Over three million beings from several species now occupied the Tortuga system, all dedicated to eradicating the synth lords. Those that didn't fight worked long hours to support those that did. At this rate they might have a real chance at winning... eventually.

"The wreckage of the synth lord destroyer did provide us

some insight into synth technology." Drake continued. "We now have upgraded computers and weapon systems though the ADE system requires a slow and methodical development process that disallows making a standard part of the designs. After your use of the multi cannon antimatter dissolution emitters the systems that are in use have been upgraded to a forty-cannon system that fires a salvo each ninety seconds after warming up in programmable preset patterns. This system has also been integrated into the dreadnaught designs expected to be deployed within five years and, of course, The battle cruiser *Jack Ketch III* which is almost complete. The system still takes over ten minutes to firing status, but we have people working around the clock to overcome that challenge."

Drake looked at the floor a moment before making his final statement.

"All we are waiting for to begin operations is your approval. We stand ready to fight for you Jax."

After Drakes report the Cthichek reported on the home defense system which had been woefully inadequate when faced with a single synth destroyer. Minefields and floating defense platforms now scattered the Tortuga system with high powered gravity well engines ready to throw enemy starships directly into the quasar. The cthichek were learning war.

Ja'Zhara reported on new assault armor capable of acting as micro starships to allow boarding without having to directly dock with enemy craft. The downside of such action being the time it took to cut an entry hole in black hole steel. The gharian did report being pleased with the cutting laser as a hand to hand weapon.

The andromedin reported a four hundred percent increase in trained and chipped andie personnel, raising their ability to man the growing armada. An over-all medical computer had been developed to assist medical personnel faced with caring for multi species crews. Attempts to add cybernetic suites to andie volunteers had yet to meet with success. The gharians, promach and cthichek had so far absolutely refused the experiments. The andromedin giving the report seemed upset by the last. Jax understood their reticence all too well.

Jax left the meeting feeling overwhelmed. Literally millions of beings counted on him and more joined every day. As far as he could tell the only thing stemming the tide lay in the complications of coming to the Tortuga system. Jax had already heard rumors that for every being that arrived at Tortuga there were two that didn't make it. The Milky Way corporations had cracked down on all resistance, freely executing suspected rebels. It only made matters worse as the tide of beings trying to escape grew logarithmically.

Several small uprisings had been attempted and quashed by the corporate forces using new technology provided by the synth lords. Jax had even heard of a synth/corporate armada that prowled andromedin space hunting for signs of the rebels. Two gathering stations had been found and destroyed. Thousands of incoming refugees had died before they could get word out of the compromised stations.

It was all too much. This had all begun to find freedom and it seemed each day Jax became more tied to his desk acting as the rebellion as figurehead. When it came right down to it, they had done better while he had been in

a coma while orbiting the quasar.
Perhaps that was the answer…

Jax found a com system and
called Baylee.

The viewer lit up showing
Baylee in full uniform at a
cluttered desk that had to be
bigger than the shack she had
been living in when Jax found
her. Before she could speak Jax
cut in.

"Baybay I need five crews for
my own lance. The *Jack Ketch*, a
destroyer, an andie frigate, an
armed heavy cargo unit, and a
full starship carrier. I need the
lance crewed by the most
aggressive, scurvy band of misfits
that can be found, and I want the
lance to be completely my own
from of my share of the booty.
Anything I can't afford I will pay
for from future booty. I will need

460

provisions for long term as well
as spare parts to repair battle
damage for all ships. What will it
take to make this happen?" Jax
realized he wanted this
desperately. He was drowning in
the bureaucracy of war. Making
decisions for an entire multi
species war machine simply was
not a job he felt qualified to
perform. Everyone expected him
to have the answers to
everything. He needed to get out
and do what he knew.

Jax knew pirating. He felt he
was also exceptionally good at
pirating.

Baylee was quiet for a
moment before responding to
Jax's outburst. "Jaxie we already
have your lance set up. All we
need are crew assignments and

supplies. All you had to do was ask bro."

Jax loved his little sister and told her so.

Chapter 35 – War by Committee

Jax – Human/Gharian Enclave renamed Port Royal – Administrative Complex – Tortuga System – Peiratis cluster – Andromeda Galaxy

Prime Minister Aldus stood upon the table flashing like a fireworks display. Jax figured it was the cthichek equivalent of yelling.

The translator spewed forth his words with much less force.

"You have already risked yourself once. You have suitable responsibilities here in Port

A Pirates Booty

Royal. Why would you endanger your exalted person to go back to the Milky Way? At least wait until we have an armada built befitting your station. You are practically going out there naked with only a single lance."

Jax listened quietly as the translator droned on. He did like the sound of the new name for the human/gharian and now andromedin enclave. Port Royal seemed fitting somehow.

Jax almost fell asleep as Prime Minister Aldus continued his tirade explaining regal duty and responsibility. If Jax let him, Prime Minister Aldus would drone on for the better part of a week. Time to wrap this up.

Jax stood to look Aldus straight in the four eyestalks before speaking. "No. I am

464

leaving with the lance that I have earned as a part of my booty. I have mixed species volunteers for crew which all report directly to me and only me. The other lances should be out fighting also but you can determine that according to each species share of the starships. They do nothing for the cause sitting here docked. The best defense is a good offense. Wars are not won defensively."

Queen Keera raised herself to speak, her subdued light flashes looking much calmer than Aldus' angry display. "My boy, and at less than three decades you are an infant by cthichek standards, you oversimplify the requirements of command. There will soon be tens of millions of beings here in Tortuga. What you state in such basic fashion is a tangled and knotted situation. There are no quick answers. To attempt to cover everything that is and will be needed with a flippant declaration is, well, it is simply childish. This leaving with a few ships to go play in the Milky Way is not only foolish, you are throwing away the lives of over fifteen hundred souls that have dedicated themselves to you. Does this truly sound like the act of a mature, rational person? Think about it your excellency. We have come so far at lightning speed; do you really wish to destroy it now? We should wait and build until we are ready."

In many ways Queen Keely was right. The problem was the wait. Cthichek would be willing to wait for centuries. To the cthichek mind hiding out and hoping the problem would go away made perfect sense. Jax believed the synth lords would not wait that long and their vengeance would be terrible. Jax knew to the very core of his being he was right in this. They had to move now, even if they weren't completely ready. Big armadas meant big targets. The best way to begin harassing the corporations and the synth lords lay in quick in and out starship guerilla tactics. They had come up with the lance style starship formations while he had been healing and they were right. Cut off support and you starved the beast. With the limited resources available compared to the synth empire, it was the only path to success Jax could see.

The leader of the andromedins, Chancellor Sequoia, merely leaned in toward the table to speak. His orchestrated voice filled the air with music. "We the andromedin peoples are in agreement with the revered cthichek, though for differing reasons. As a species we have been killed, maimed, tortured, and cast from our homes by the synth lords and their corporations. Our planets have been stripped and left barren in the name of profit and power. To date we have been ineffective in our defiance, for we did not have the technology or the knowledge to effectively fight back. We have been gifted with access to the technology," at this

468

point Sequoia gave a nod toward the other members of the room, "and we have access to knowledge chips which we have recently been able to modify for our physiology. For this boon we must thank each of the species in the freedom alliance. We can now fight back. But we have no wish to nip at the heels of our enemies. We will destroy them root and stem. We will eradicate them so that nothing remains but a footnote in dusty archives. To do this we need power the like of which this universe has never seen. Super dreadnoughts to dominate the stars, armadas of thousands to impose freedom upon the native species and pluck the weeds that are our persecutors so that they may

469

understand the grievous harm
they have so carelessly wrought
upon us. Less is not more. More
is more. We have laid our plans
so that within twenty years we
shall have the instruments of our
vengeance. Within forty years we
shall have everything we could
need to remove this plague. Forty
years is not a long time compared
to the centuries of abuse we have
endured. We do not nip, we
bite!"

Hed drifted to the table. The
promach did not have a leader as
far as Jax could tell. Many hadn't
even bothered taking up
individual names yet. Almost all
the original members of the
thirteenth family of the promach
still went by Hed. The name had
become so popular Jax suspected
that many of the immigrant

470

promach had taken the name.
This also meant you could never
really tell which one you were
speaking to.

Guiding his enviro-suit to
float beside Aldus of the cthichek,
Hed began. "We have recently
acquired significant sections of
the synth computer system, no
thanks to the bull in a china shop
Captain Jax's overzealous
destruction of the scat chewing
synth box of bolts scrap heap.
With the smoking hunks of junk
retrieved from that debris, we
have been able to reverse
engineer technologies we had not
known were possible. We can
now upgrade our computer
systems over five hundred
percent. Five hundred freakin'
percent! This means we have mo'

powah. Mo powah means better software. Better software means we don't get hacked and our own systems turned against us. In that last encounter the Thrace be damned synth hackers came within a camel's armpit hair of subverting our battle computers. Without the masterful on the fly coding of over a hundred brave warriors of the thirteenth family, promach for those of you that are intelligence challenged, we would have gone down like a human virgin at a family reunion. No one had time to fight back. Another few minutes and they would have pwned every system in the fleet making all our shiny new starships their franging little illegitimate ass warts. Until we can develop defenses to better ward against computer hacking

472

from the synth, we will be as vulnerable as deaf boys carrying a bottle of lube in a pedophile monastery. We need flaerking time to build the hardware and software required to level the playing field."

Ja'Zhara looked around the room before deciding he needed to speak for the gharians. No less than seven little gharians hung about his body playing at mock battles and snapping at any being they felt got too close.

"I am Ja'Zhara, first of the free gharians. You all talk too much. We gharians fight. Alone or with you talkers does not matter. We fight." Satisfied with his speech, Ja'Zarha turned and stepped back to lean against the wall, his mace like tail curled in close.

They were right. With time the rebellion could build fleets that could defy the Milky Way Corporations and the synth lords head on.

Jax knew they didn't have the time. He wasn't sure why they had not been atacked by a squadron of synth warships already. Whatever the reason, this respite couldn't last much longer. For the rebellion to survive they needed to get spread out. Hit them at any weak spot that could be found. Low hanging fruit tasted just as sweet. If they were lucky, they could keep the synth occupied enough for the rebellion to have a chance to make the great armadas and super dreadnaughts described.

The starship attack lance remained their best chance to take the fight to the enemy on his own turf. Battle damage from both sides weakened the enemy's infrastructure. Even better, any resources they could take from the enemy weakened them and strengthened the rebellion. Just as wolves took down great elk, the lances could take down synth warships one at a time. It was the only way they could effectively fight against such a huge foe with the resources they had right now. They needed to send out every lance and warship as soon as possible to cause as much mayhem and destruction as they could. Weaken the synth and corporate infrastructure even as they strengthened their own.

A Pirates Booty

Jax refused to ask others to do what he would not.

There was only one argument left.

Jax declared loudly for all to hear. "I invoke the fealty of all who swore to follow my commands as stated."

Everything after that was just paperwork and posturing. This soul fealty had its uses. Jax would never admit it to Ally or Baylee though. They would become insufferable.

Besides, he had a shiny new ship without a single scratch to try out.

Chapter 29 – Return to the Cold Black

*Jax – The Jack Ketch III –
Outside Turtuga system – Peiratis
cluster – Andromeda Galaxy*

Once he had put his foot down things had moved remarkably quickly. By the end of the week the crew were settled in and going about their duties. Leaving port seemed a bit anticlimactic as they simply disengaged and left. From what Jax could see they weren't the only lance leaving port. Several had left before his own lance and many more were in the process of preparing to leave.

Jax's lance proved to be the pride of the fleet. The *Jack Ketch III* had six overpowered ftl engines with a forty ADE cannon array that could fire in a two hundred seventy-degree arc. Four ten-ton drone missile tubes had been added as well as six entire banks of Focused Anti-Matter Stream generators and Fermian Discharge Cannons. Smaller laser and photon defense canons covered the ship like a blanket.

Drake's *Gold Digger* had been scrapped and rebuilt with seven hard points consisting of an additional five kinetic cannon and three each Anti Matter Dissolution Emmiter generators and Fermian Discharge cannons.

The twelve, twenty-ton drone missile tubes could send a barrage of a dozen missiles every minute as long as the missiles lasted. The *Gold Digger II* could dominate a battle with sheer firepower.

Allie commanded the *Valkyrie*, one of the new super carriers. The separating cluster design had been scrapped for a flying support starship carrying a complete hospital, repair bay, industrial parts printers, and the most powerful sensor suite that they had been able to make. Oh, and it had a compliment of a hundred starfighters with twenty spares.

Maddie captained the hauler of her dreams. Thirty standard engines and twenty ftl engines meant the *Kraken II* could keep up with all but the fastest starships while towing over a hundred fully loaded tow crates. With a fore hull of ten-foot-thick black hole steel and a triple layered shielding system the Kraken no longer depended on other craft for protection. As a bonus, the *Kraken* towed two full crates of spare fighters that could be launched within twenty minutes, crate to space.

The smallest of the lance, the andromedin frigate *Morning Glory* had systems Jax had never heard of. The Andies had gone with every new weapon system they could devise in their embrace of new technology. It remained to be seen how effective the ship would be, but Jax figured a wild card in battle couldn't hurt.

All in all, with this lance, mostly captained by his closest friends, Jax felt ready to take on the galaxy.

The freedom rebellion had become more than a few ragtag ships running for their lives. Jax burned with pride in his people. Not just the humans or cyborgs, but all his people, of whatever species. No matter where this ended, they stood together at this moment to defy the injustice of the universe.

Powering up the control hologram, Jax set parameters for the training engagement. The battle of Tortuga had taught everyone the value of knowing your equipment, so Jax kept constant simulations and mock battles running for anyone that had a spare moment. Since the crew had been able to offer suggestions to the specific systems of their starship, the controls ran much smoother than previous versions. Even his command hologram felt more natural, like an extension of Jax's thought process. The rebuilt and upgraded *Jack Ketch III* responded like a set of powered armor as it glided according to Jax's whim.

Great compatriots, a solid ship around him and the vastness of space as his playground. What more could a pirate want?

The cocoa wasn't bad either.

From the Author

Bill – Yuma, Arizona In USA of North America – Earth – Sol system – Orion-Cygnus Arm between the Sagittarius and the Perseus Arms – Milky Way Galaxy

Thank you, dear reader, for once again delving the fables of the spacefaring buccaneers and the adventures of Captain Jax and the crew of the *Jack Ketch*. This book took longer than expected and for your patience I am profoundly grateful. Since I don't do a lot of the things required to market my books, I am always surprised at how well they have been received. For your very kind

A Pirates Booty

words and steadfast patronage I
humbly thank you. Look on for a
taste of the next book in this
series "*The Captains Share*"

Excerpt from The

Captains Share

Captain Allie – Podunk –
Shepard Spur – Milky Way Galaxy

"*J*ax better know what he is doing! Arrgh! The things I let that man talk me into!" Allie mumbled to herself as she watched her star fighters launch by twos into the space surrounding the planet Podunk. All the training had paid off as the entire group gathered in perfect formation beyond the super carrier, *Valkyrie*'s, bow. With a hundred starfighters and her carrier, Jax had asked her to

A Pirates Booty

hold off a full destroyer lance
sent to destroy Jax's home world
for no more reason than it was
Jax's point of origin.

Her carrier and fighters were
bait in a trap Jax promised her
would give the freedom fighters a
distinct advantage. That the
expected bonanza would fatten
her share of the booty quite nicely
did play a part in her decision.

Allie growled to herself. Jax
had sweet talked her knowing
she couldn't say no to him or to
easy booty.

And there they were, right on
time. It looked like two corporate
destroyers supported by three
frigates and some corvette fast
movers. More firepower than
Allie had expected. This wasn't
going to be the walk in the park

486

Jax had promised. This was going to be hard and bloody.

Allie commed to the starfighters, "Stealth mode now. Low emission status and no communication until they have passed through your formation."

The fighters were small enough to avoid scanner detection at this range giving Allie the opportunity to try out the new stealth systems the cthichek had installed. Based on the stealth system in the original *Jack Ketch* the system had never been combat tested. Allie realized there had to be a first time for everything, but did it have to be in a major engagement?

Oddly enough, it worked. As soon as the warships passed the fighter powered up all systems and dove in guns blazing. The corvettes were the first to go, followed almost immediately by one of the frigates. Every ship they could take down before the corporate starships could regroup and fight back increased her chances of getting through this with minimal damage.

The corporate destroyers came fully online as the second frigate blew apart in a fiery mass leaving a single frigate and the two destroyers.

Much better odds

Better odds until the three synth frigates came into sensor range moving at an unheard-of speed in system of 3.4 lightyears per minute.

Allie was well and truly screwed, and not in the happy

"Jax scoot over now" kind of way.

A Pirates Booty

Appendixes

Appendix I – Species

Andromedin – aka Andies

Group – Grove
Young – Sapling
Males – Stoma
Females – Hip
Nemales – N/A

Preferred
Environment

490

Andromedin planets normally range from .6 to 2.5 human standard gravities. While andromedins require the highest oxygen levels of the known intelligent species they are very resistant to trace elements that are usually poisonous to other species. Andromedins do well on temperate planets (70° F to 90° F) but can survive in temperatures from – 60° F to 160° F. Andromedins do require at least three hours of solar energy per cycle for survival with ten to fifteen hours being preferred.

Physical Traits

491

A Pirates Booty

As master of the medical sciences, Andromedins often adjust their base DNA to create andromedin versions of other species. Unadjusted, the physical standard for andromedins are short legged, bipedal creatures. Standard height runs from 78 inches to 128 inches with weights from five hundred to eighteen hundred pounds for males or females.

Procreation is completed anytime two andromedins come within ten feet when one or more males release tiny spores which are captured by small cilia on any females in range. This occurs naturally and without conscious thought from the andromedins themselves.

The andromedin body consists of a wide cylindrical torso that makes up over 75% of their height. The two arms and two legs end in knotty club like appendages with four to ten metatarsals extruding. The upper metatarsals are used for manipulating objects. The sensor array in a large knot above the torso, much like a human head, contains the maw for ingestion as well as several sensory organs. Sensory organs include sight, hearing, barometric pressure, and air movement.

General Psychology

Andromedins normally follow a live and let live policy

493

concerning others. The depredations of the Milky Way corporations have brought out a violent viciousness that is new to their interactions with other species. Andromedins are fiercely loyal to friends and unforgiving enemies. Because of the nature of their communication, Andromedins do not understand lies since they cannot lie to each other. This also makes crime in andromedin society almost nonexistent since guilt or innocence can be determined by simply asking. When for crime is meted out, it is usually considered over harsh by other species. i.e. Theft of an item considered to be valued over one year's wages normally gets a death sentence with the

494

perpetrators dna removed from the gene pool.

Longevity of andromedins is not known but is estimated to be two to five hundred years.

Organization

The best way to describe andromedin structure would be mob rule with designated leaders chosen for specific tasks. Should a situation come up that require a leader, a leader is chosen by the andromedins involved and they continue to lead until the required function has been completed. Should long term leaders be needed for extended projects, a leader will be chosen as usual with successors being

designed and raised to perform
the specific functions necessary.

Natural
Communication
Method

Inner-species telepathy. To
communicate with other species
an andromedin must be designed
and raised to speak specific
languages.

Cthichek – aka crabs

Group – Cast
Young – Zoe
Males – Jimmy
Females – Sally
Nemales – Finley

Preferred Environment

Cthichek are the most physically hardy of the known sentient species. Cthichek planets normally range from 0 to 100 human standard gravities while preferred gravitational pull seems to be about two gravities. Cthichek do well swimming in

A Pirates Booty

the ammonia oceans of gas giants
as well as the sparce atmosphere
of small moons. Cthichek also
have an amazing resistance to
temperature extremes have been
known to thrive in the bitter cold
of helium oceans (-500° F) to the
blistering heat of near solar
planets (500° F) While cthichek
can survive in extreme heat they
find it uncomfortable. A traveling
salesman managed to sell the
cthichek butter to drench
themselves in when overheated
and the cthichek now reference
"butter weather" for areas too hot
for comfort. Cthichek are also the
only species capable of
withstanding the pressures and
temperatures required to make
black hole steel.

498

Physical Traits

Cthichek have both an inner skeleton as well as an exoskeleton. An oval body will normally have ten appendages. Only the two front appendages are used to manipulate objects. At the front of the body four eyestalks are used for sight, two for close detailed work and two for distance vision. Cthicheck have no sense of hearing but do have and added seismic organs on their feet that sense vibration well enough to feel footsteps of a human from over two hundred yards.

Cthichek never stop growing, so standard size runs from one-inch tall and seven-inch diameter for young adults, to three-foot tall

499

and twelve-foot diameter for ancients. Diameter is measured from claw tip to claw tip.

General
Psychology

"It wasn't me" should be the clarion call for the cthichek. To avoid responsibility the cthichek culture has developed a complex social system where blame for each activity is assigned much like punishment. This has become such a basic part of the cthichek psyche that extreme safety measures are installed in all cthichek engineered equipment to avoid responsibility for accidents.

Cthichek are tri sexed with males, females and nemales. Procreation consists of a ritualistic joining wherein the nemales takes the sperm of the male and the egg of the female to build a hard shell surrounding the new life. Nemales are also responsible for breaking away this shell when the zoea are hatched since the shell is much too hard for the newborn to crack on its own. Care and feeding of the newborn is shared by all three parents until the young cthicheck is ready to enter society as an adult.

Organization

Cthichek are ruled by a triumvirate that consists of the

eldest member of each sex. Rules
for administration are very
specific and can be extremely
rigid to avoid unanticipated
blame.

Natural Communication Method

Cthichek communicate using
colored light pulses emanating
from the back of their carapace.

Gharians – no standard

reference beyond normal

Group – Lounge

Young – Hatchling

Males – Bull

Females – Saurus

Nemales – N/A

*Preferred
Environment –*

Gharian planets closely match human standards with a range from .2 to 3 human standard gravities, preferred gravitational pull almost exactly matches human at 1.07 standard gravities. True to their reptilian physiology, gharians prefer temperate, humid

503

planets. The comfort range for gharian covers 80° F to 130° F with humidity over 60 percent. Gharians become lethargic at lower temperatures but can survive for short periods in extreme cold. Temperatures exceeded 140° F are not survivable for gharians.

Physical Traits -

Standard height for a gharian male ranges from eight foot six inches to eleven feet while upright females range from twenty feet to twenty-eight feet tall. Although capable, females rarely travel upright. The reptilian body shape includes a tail with a bony club at the end for balance. Arms and legs are roughly proportional to human norms for males, though the females have arms that are proportional to the legs for quadrupedal movement. A gharians head is more like a tyrannosaurus shape than an alligator. Hard scales cover most of the gharians bodies with smaller scales covering inner joints and the underbelly. A single hard plate covers the head which carries similar sensory organs to humans. Gharians do have an added magnetic sense derived from nodules set into their jaw line.

Reproduction occurs when the males are gifted with an egg from the female which he then fertilized and nurtures to adulthood. Females rarely interact with gharian young.

General Psychology

Gharians center their existence around familial lounges. An adult female will call for males when she has reached an age for mating. Young females will have two or three male consorts while elder females can have as many as twenty males in their stable. Males have a single opportunity for placement in a female's lounge which will be determined by combat. Prior to modern medicine, most

unsuccessful males died during
the competition. With the advent
of medical breakthroughs that
healed more and more of the
losing combatants, an entire
clique of casteless male
developed which became the
spacefaring arm of the gharians.

Organization

Though specific governance
can be of any type, Gharian
society follows a strongly
matriarchal culture.

Natural Communication
method – Gharians communicate
using sound issued from their
voice box much as humans do.
They are physically incapable of

A Pirates Booty

reproducing human speech
though and must use translators.

Humans – aka

Spewmonkeys (vulgar insult used only by the cthichek of the thirteenth family) Meat Sacks (Vulgar insult used by the Synth Lords though this may be used to denote any biological)

Group – Crowd or mob

Young – Children

Males – Man

Females – Woman

Nemales – N/A

Physical Traits

Standard human size ranges from five foot to seven-foot-tall for adult males and four foot six

A Pirates Booty

inches to just over six feet for
adult females. Weights range
from 90 pounds to over six
hundred pounds.

General
Psychology

Humans be crazy

Organization

Randomly, and usually
ineffectively, organized

Natural
Communication
method

Humans communicate using
sound. Galactic common is a

variant of human speech adjusted
for gharian use.

Promach – aka Snot-balls

(*vulgar insult*)

Group – Family
Young – Stellaris
Males – Stairn
Females – Nes
Nemales – N/A

Preferred Environment

Promach prefer low or no gravity areas of space such as small moons or even asteroid belts. Comfortable temperature for promach ranges from -100° F to -150° F. Of the known intelligent species promach are the most frail, unable to

512

withstand even a single human standard gravity or more than a ten percent variance from their comfortable temperature range. For this reason, promach have developed some of the best environmental suits and gravity dampeners in the known universe.

Physical Traits

Promach are an amorphous species with a surface tension just below that of water. Adult promach weigh between a pound and three pounds. Promach procreate through merging with another to share enough dna and material to create a new young promach with traits and

513

knowledge derived from the
donor, or a single promach may
reproduce using fission which
creates two promach with the
exact same memories and traits
as the original.

General
Psychology

Promach are divided into
twelve families which rarely
interact. A thirteenth family has
recently been added. Promach are
very algorithmic thinker and do
things in a predefined pattern.
The lends them toward many of
the engineering fields and they
make the best software engineers
in existence. Sensitive to their
wea constitution when compared
to other sentient species, promach

are often loud and can often be considered rude and brusque (esp. the newly formed thirteenth family). Promach lack much of a sense of individualism preferring to live as a part of the whole family.

Natural Communication Method

Promach communicate using light pulses emitted from within their body, much like deep sea creature's bioluminescence.

A Pirates Booty

Synth Lords – aka

(every curse word known to any sentient species)

Group – Congress
Young – N/A
Males – N/A
Females – N/A
Nemales – N/A

Physical Traits

As each synth lord has been designed by the parent synth, physical traits vary widely. Synth also make copies of themselves which can be of any size of shape.

516

General
Psychology

Synth lords are arrogant and cruel in any interaction with other species. Synth look down upon biological beings as being beneath them, suitable only for mundane tasks and amusement. With each other the synth are extremely competitive, constantly working to show themselves as a better design. Failure is intolerable in the synth society as is any form of weakness. Alliances and governing bodies change at the whim of the individual synth making synth politics ever changing. Synth procreate when an elder synth wishes to showcase its abilities by

517

creating a more advanced
artificial intelligence.

Synth all agree that a single
synth lord's interests and life are
valued far beyond any other
entire species.

Organization

Synth rule over their chosen
are like the fiefdoms of old. Synth
will not tolerate other synths
having any kind of dominance so
attempts to create an overall
synth government have been
doomed to failure.

Natural
Communication
Method

Spacefaring Buccaneer Series

Synth can use every known
communication method.

A Pirates Booty

Appendix II – Cast of Players

Andromedi

n

Dr. Regis Quercus – 8′ 2″ 1200 lbs– First andromedin to receive the reed and flute organs to naturally mimic human speech. Known expert on human and cyborg biology.

Chancellor Azaella Sequoia – 9′ 6″ 1435 lbs. First chosen andromedin to take the duties of leading the freedom rebellion for the andromedin species.

Captain Jariste Prosopis – 7′ 10″, 1080 lbs. Captain of the Morning Glory. First Captain of the budding Andromedin fleet

Cthichek

Glixen aka "Crab Man" – 2' 11" tall, 9' 6" diameter. The first cthichek Jax ever met. A key being in the initial escape from Arrex Ten

General Raspit – 2' 5" tall, 7' 3" diameter – Leader of the Tortuga Cthichek Defense force

Queen Keera – 2' 6" tall, 9' 11" diameter, Matriarchal leader of the Tortuga Cthichek

Prime Minister Aldus – 3' 2" tall, 11' 3" diameter – Patriarchal leader of the Tortuga Cthichek

Fornai – 1' 10" tall, 5' 6" diameter – Handmaiden to the queen

Serpio – 2' 1" tall, 9' 4" diameter – Chief Beaurocrat

A Pirates Booty

Vareyan – 1' 10" tall, 6' 4"
diameter – Royal Cthichek
Warden for Tortuga

Gharian

Ja'Zhara aka "Big Green" 9'
7" 1650 lbs – The first gharian Jax
ever interacted with. Leader of
the gharian contingent of the
freedom fighters.

Human

Captain Jax Morgan – 6' 5"
355lbs (Cyborg) – Bawndonk
Village, Podunk, Shepards Spur,
Milky Way – Leader of the
rebellion.
Captain Drake Jaxson 6' 0'
316 lbs (Cyborg) – Jax's close
friend since becoming an indent.

Captain Allie Adamanche 5' 10" 295 lbs. (Cyborg) – Jax's closest friend since becoming an indentured slave. After a rocky, and violent, beginning Jax's girlfriend.

Amaleen Morgan 5' 5" 135 lbs – Jax's mother. Spent her entire life as a scrub farmer on Podunk in the Milky Way. Died from poverty while Jax was serving his indenture.

Ryken Morgan 6' 3" 225 lbs. – Jax's brother. Blamed for his mother's abject poverty when he stole the tax money to move to the big city. Killed by local security forces during the escape from Podunk.

Joli Morgan 5' 7" 130 lbs – Jax's sister. Believed dead from

A Pirates Booty

narcotic overdose while Jax
served his indenture.

Baylee Morgan 5′ 3″ 126 lbs –
Jax's only known surviving
relative. Acts as purser for the
freedom rebellion. Developed the
booty system as it is used today.

Carmen 5″ 5″ 275 lbs.
(Cyborg) – Shanghaied Jax to
begin his indenture. Later
indentured for cause to become a
cyborg of Peadee Five. Died in
the battle of Tortuga.

Phelan 5′ 10″ 305 lbs.–
Shanghaied Jax to begin his
indenture. Later indentured for
cause to become a cyborg of
Peadee Five.

Fleke (or Fleek) 5′4″ 125 lbs. –
Hacker picked up on Podunk

Dr. Carmen Savage 5′ 7″ 190
lbs. – Doctor picked up in the big
city of Podunk

Dr. Claudeburge – 5"9" 275 lbs. Doctor picked up in the big city of Podunk

Cooter – 5' 6" 155 lbs – (Real name unknown) – Starship mechanic and general fixit engineer. Ran the spaceport in Jax's hometown until joining Jax in his escape.

Promach

Hed (Hacker Epsilon David) – 12 oz, 4-inch diameter when all pseudopods are retracted – The first promach Jax ever met. Met while indentured to Arrex Ten. Masterminded the escape that led to their freedom.

Also Hed – Most of the promach in the thirteenth family.

A Pirates Booty

Though as of this writing they are beginning to determine a more specific naming structure.

Hab (Hacker Aileen Bravo) – 9 oz, 3.7-inch diameter when all pseudopods are retracted – The promach that attached to Drake

Synth Lords

Arrex Ten – Relatively new member of synth lord society. The synth that bought Jax, Allie, and Drake when they became 3C indents. Experimented on all three to add new synth technology to find what it considered the perfect blend. Killed during their escape to freedom.

Spacefaring Buccaneer Series

Peadee Five – Arrex Ten's progenitor. Searches for the freedom rebellion to crush it into oblivion.

Ennwun – Elder of the Synth Lord peoples. First to attack Peadee Ten for incompetence.

A Pirates Booty

Appendix III – Personal Weaponry

Slug thrower – A rifle or pistol relatively unchanged since the old west on earth

Magnetic Rail Cannon – A cannon or rifle that cuts sections of gauged wire to accelerate along the barrel using a magnetic rail.

Quark multiplier – A cannon, rifle or pistol that sends an energized quark beam to the target.

Electron charge emitter – A pistol that send a controlled electric charge to the target. Not considered a line of sight weapon.

Scrambler – A weapon addon that sends a pulse of varied

control frequencies to scramble computer control systems.

Neural shock field generator – A cannon, rifle, or pistol designed to shock the system of biologicals for capture.

Microdrone Launcher – A Cannon, rifle, or pistol that launches drones at the target, Drones are designed for specific purposes, such as seek and destroy or surveillance, but multiple types of drones may be used in the same launcher.

Appendix IV – Ship Weaponry

Energy Weapons

Focused Multi Beam Laser – Cannon that allows short precise bursts of fire. Used on smaller ships or to remove particles from the flight path.

Quark Multiplier Cannons (Quarkies, Quarms) – Cannon that allows continuous fire. Used on smaller ships or to remove particles from the flight path.

Focused Solar Flare Cannon (FSF) – Midsized canon used mostly by the promach.

Gravitex (Thumpers)– A large cannon sends a cannonball

shaped gravity distortion that distorts gravity in the area around it. Limited use in standard space battle tactics.

Fusion Accelerators (Fas)–Heavy beam weapon. Kills things dead. Not effective at super light speeds

Focused Anti-Matter Stream (Slap Bangs) - Dangerous beam weapon (explodes easy) Used on most capitol warships

Fermian Discharge Cannon (Ferns) – Mid level beam cannon usable at super light speeds

Antimatter Dissolution Emitters – Devastating beam weapon, though power up time is

A Pirates Booty

excessive and recharge rate is
slow

Kinetic:
5 Ton Drone Missile – Holds a
dozen prepackaged drones
10 Ton Drone Missile – Holds
up to twenty-five prepackaged
drones
20 Ton Drone Missile – Holds
up to fifty prepackaged drones
50 Ton Drone Missile – Holds
up to one hundred prepackaged
capital drones

Engine Emitter Drone – Acts
as a tiny remote-controlled
spaceship
Attack Drone (Energy) – Acts
as a self-controlled drone using
quark multiplier guns or focused
lasers to attack.

Attack Drone (Kinetic) – Acts as a self-controlled drone using mag rail guns to attack.

Attack Drone (Dumb) – Acts as a self-controlled drone self-destructing on impact with target.

Defense Drone (Scatter shot) – Acts as a self-controlled drone to desensitize scanners in an area and break weapon lock.

Defense Drone (ECM) – Acts as a self-controlled drone used to assist hackers also used to corrupt computer system commands.

Single Attack Missiles – Used to fire and forget, these weapons have been phased out because of poor performance and holding space requirements.

533

A Pirates Booty

Rail Guns – Sends a huge chunk of solid metal at target.

Scatter shot cannon – Spreads small pieces of material in a cloud to desensitize scanners and weapon lock.

Appendix V – Asexual, Third, and

Fourth sex pronouns

Style	Male	Female Asexual
Subject		
	He	She It
Object		
	Him It	Her
Possessive		

534

His	Her	Its

Possessive Pronoun

	His	Hers
	Its	

Reflexive

	Himself	Herself
	itself	

Style	**Group *Nemale**	
	**Veme	

Subject

They	Ne	Ve

Object

Them	Nem	Ver

535

A Pirates Booty

Possessive

| Their | Nir | Vis |

Possessive Pronoun

| Theirs | Nirs | Vis |

Reflexive

Themselves   Nemself
        Verself

*Denotes the third cthichek sex

** Denotes Non-Understood or undefinable sexual reference

Appendix VI – Indentured Service Classifications

3C – A class 3C indenture requires a five to ten year contract. Work performed may not be any more dangerous than freemen though working hours may be longer and no time off needs to be given by the owner. Indents of this class can expect to be in good health at the end of their term. A stipend upon successful completion of term is normally offered.

3B – A class 3B indenture requires a ten to twenty year contract. Work performed may not be any more dangerous than freemen though working hours may be longer and no time off needs to be given by the owner. Indents of this class can expect to be in good health at the end of their term. A stipend upon successful completion of term is normally offered.

3A – A class 3A indenture requires a contract over twenty years. Work performed may not be any more dangerous than freemen though working hours may be longer and no time off needs to be given by the owner. Indents of this class can expect to be in good health at the end of their term. A stipend consisting of a monthly account upon successful completion of term is normally offered

2C – A class 2C indenture requires a ten year contract from date of inception. Previous time spent as a level 1 indent is not taken into account. Work performed may not be immediately dangerous but may have long term or "accidental" risks to health and sanity. At the end of their term indents are sometime provided health care to repair mental and physical damage that occurred during their term. Upon completion of contract the indent will be discharged at a location containing at least one hundred of their own species at the convenience of the contract holder.

2B – A class 2B indenture requires a twenty year contract from date of inception. Previous time spent as a level 1 indent is not taken into account. Work performed may not be immediately dangerous but may have long term or "accidental" risks to health and sanity. At the end of their term indents are sometime provided health care to repair mental and physical damage that occurred during their term. Upon completion of contract the indent will be discharged at a location containing at least ten of their own species at the convenience of the contract holder.

2A – A class 2A indenture requires a lifetime contract from date of inception. A lifetime is measured by the time that the indent can continue to provide useful service. Work performed may not be immediately dangerous but may have long term or "accidental" risks to health and sanity. At the end of their term indents are sometime provided health care to repair mental and physical damage that occurred during their term. Upon completion of contract the indent will be discharged at the convenience of the contract holder.

1C – A class 1C indenture requires a ten year contract. Any work or testing that shows a benefit to the Milky Way Galaxy coalition may be performed by or on the indent. Disposal of the indent at the end of their term is up to the contract holder.

1B – A class 1B indenture requires a twenty year contract.

A Pirates Booty

Any work or testing may be
performed by or on the indent.
Disposal of the indent at the end
of their term is up to the contract
holder.

1A – A class 1A indenture is
permanent. Indents under this
type of contract may be used or
modified for any reason. Disposal
of the remains are the
responsibility of the contract
holder.

Made in the USA
Monee, IL
04 November 2020